Praise for

"For such a slim book,
Subtle, difficult, lov
—*KIRKUS REVI*

"Pung delicately teases out the common experience of a daughter resenting her mother and looking up to her father, made even more complex by fraught racial dynamics."
—*THE GUARDIAN*

"Pung shines when conveying the feelings of a child whose adulthood is fast approaching, and the emotions of a mother who is losing control."—*THE WASHINGTON POST*

"Throughout, Pung effectively channels her protagonist's restless outlook. This is worth checking out."
—*PUBLISHERS WEEKLY*

"A powerhouse story, a powerhouse voice, that wrestles with intragenerational fractures and complicated entanglements. At the center of the book is an obsessive kind of love, a love that gives but also takes, but a love that only forms from bonds forged in fire."
—WEIKE WANG, AWARD-WINNING AUTHOR OF
JOAN IS OKAY AND *CHEMISTRY*

"Alice Pung's *One Hundred Days* is a searingly intimate portrait of a fight for selfhood in a culturally complex family. As much as Karuna Kelly is writing to her baby about to be born, she's also trying to discern who to trust: her controlling mother or her absent father, her well-intentioned but distant teachers or the intrusive government officials who claim to be trying to help? I was riveted by Pung's lyrical prose in which separation is a threat that benefits and wounds at surprising turns."
—JIMIN HAN, AUTHOR OF
THE APOLOGY AND *A SMALL REVOLUTION*

ONE HUNDRED DAYS

Also by Alice Pung

Unpolished Gem
Growing up Asian in Australia (ed.)
Her Father's Daughter
Laurinda
My First Lesson (ed.)
Writers on Writers: Alice Pung on John Marsden
Close to Home: Selected Writings

FOR CHILDREN
Meet Marly
Marly's Business
Marly and the Goat
Marly Walks on the Moon
When Granny Came to Stay
Be Careful, Xiao Xin!
Millie Mak the Maker

ONE
HUNDRED
DAYS

ALICE PUNG

HarperVia

An Imprint of HarperCollinsPublishers

I celebrate myself...
And what I assume you shall assume
For every atom belonging to me as good belongs to you.

Walt Whitman

Prologue

Ever since your Grand Par left, your Grand Mar and I share the double bed. She says she can't sleep by herself, that it's too dark, even though the hallway light shines on the stippled cement dots on our ceiling. It's like an asphalt galaxy up there, like the road is above us instead of fourteen floors below.

I hate sleeping with your Grand Mar. In the months after your Grand Par left, she used to work herself up into such a state that her chest heaved like engine pistons going up and down, up and down, like the organs inside the ribcages of the cars your Grand Par showed me. I once saw a documentary about a woman who could only breathe through iron lungs. She was part-machine, a horizontal robot that was half-deflated. That is how your Grand Mar was in those early days, a sad sack of skin bagging a mechanical-breakdown chest.

Your Grand Mar always said that if I had been a son, then he would've stayed. "Boys belong to their fathers, girls belong to their mothers," she'd tell me, which would really piss me off because I didn't want to belong to anyone.

It would be nice if I could start off with a fairytale, something that makes you think that the world is much bigger than us beneath our ceiling. But it's just me and you and your Grand

Mar and the dark, and even though I would like to begin anywhere but here, here is where I am and where you start.

In the dark there is no big bad wolf, even though your Grand Mar wants to wring his name out of me. In fairytales the princess stays silent, because if she blurts out even one syllable, snakes fall from her mouth, or the kingdom collapses, or her firstborn is doomed. As for the hero prince, well, he can say whatever he likes; worlds never crumble when he rabbits on. Sometimes the beast and the prince are the same person, but you will find these things out for yourself, I think.

I know your Grand Mar stares at me in the blackness. I can feel her head turning on her pillow, and then she asks, "Who is it?"

When I don't answer, she says, "Do you even know who it is? Because if you don't know who it is, we can get the police to look for them and catch them and lock them away." She says this to me like I am five years old and don't know about the law. "In jail," she adds.

When I still won't talk, she mutters, "Never knew any girl could be so dumb."

I am not dumb, even though I know your Grand Mar thinks this every time I make a decision that has nothing to do with her. She has to say yes or no to every thought of mine, and it gets harder and harder to have secret thoughts since we share the same bed and she bugs me every night, but I have this notebook and she can't read what I write even if she opens it (which she has) and grills me about it (which she also has). "Just practising my writing," I tell her, which is not a lie at all, "for when I go back to school," which we both know is a lie.

When she is not in such a dark-dark mood, she is even patient and cajoling. "You can tell your Mar," she says. "You know I want to help you. You will not get into any trouble if you let me know." I hate this even more than her anger. I know she will go back on her word, that I will not only get myself into trouble but your dad too.

I say nothing, and predictably, after a few seconds, she falls back into her angry state, sizzling and hissing like water on a hotplate.

"Will it be a Ghost baby or a human baby?" she spits.

I say nothing.

Being so close to her makes me curl up inside myself like a cashew. Your Grand Mar wishes she could have known about you when you were the size of a nut, because then she could have found a way to shake you from your shell. But even I didn't know about you then.

Your Grand Mar is not the only one who says I am stupid. They look at me like I'm a caged bunny that escaped and got myself into a bad state, all soft paws and silent yowls. But your father was not a criminal. He was just a boy I liked, and then he left, but by then you were here.

And like some mythical monster, I now have two heartbeats.

"Listen, can you hear that, Karuna? That's your baby's heartbeat," Dr Masano said, when she first put the fetoscope to my stomach. I'd waited too long to see the doctor, so the first time I heard you, you were a loud and frantic throb.

"It's scared," I told her. "That's why its heart is beating so fast." Before you'd even begun, I felt like I'd stuffed up, stuffed you full of my own fears.

She laughed. "No, don't worry, the reason the heartbeat is so fast is because the baby's so tiny. It's the size of a passion fruit."

Ha, I thought, passion fruit. I remembered all those Hail Marys at Christ Our Saviour College, kneeling during confession, trying to keep a straight face at "fruit of thy womb". When your Grand Par left, he took that faith with him as well, because that was the end of my private school education.

Now, lying in the dark with your Grand Mar next to me, depressing half the bed and all of my life, I can only wait for you to come and shake things up.

And the one hundred days have only just begun.

Then

Chapter 1

They all think that things changed for me when I got knocked up, but they don't know that it started much, much earlier. It used to be that I thought one thing at a time, but that summer, the hottest we'd had in a while, my thoughts became scattered. Instead of marching in military formation through my mind, they dithered and loitered and looked in different windows. I had to keep chasing after them, which made it difficult for me to remember practical things – like bringing in the laundry before it rained, peeling carrots and finishing my history homework.

The school chaplain told me it probably had something to do with sudden changes in my life beyond my control, like your Grand Par leaving, but I knew that wasn't it. It had started happening way before that.

Your Grand Mar always had great expectations of me. Because she didn't have many small things when she was growing up, she made me her Big Thing. It was both deliberate and accidental, the way most important decisions are. Like you. Until the summer I turned thirteen, I hadn't realised that she had

been narrating the story of my life, including the dialogue.
Until then, I believed her fairytales, because I was at the centre
of them.

This is how your Grand Mar tells it: one day she was walking around End Point Shopping Centre with me in the pram
when she was stopped by a woman. The woman had a booth in
the middle of the mall, between a stall that sold imitation Lisa
Frank stationery and a Wendy's.

"Your baby is so beautiful!" the woman cooed. She pointed
to a small platform she had set up, draped in white satin, against
a plastic backdrop of cumulus clouds. A tinsel halo jutted out
from a piece of wire at the top like a basketball hoop.

"I don't have any money," your Grand Mar muttered, steer-
ing the pram away.

"No, no, I'd like to take her photo for free! For free!"

Your Grand Mar reluctantly handed me over. A camera
stood on a tripod like a ginormous insect waiting to sting.

I think I must have been picked simply because of my
outfit, a second-hand christening gown that your Grand Mar
had shortened so that it ended at my feet instead of hanging
half a metre below. With the leftover cotton and lace she had
made me a little cape with flouncy cap sleeves. Your Grand
Mar was good with her Singer, transforming op-shop dresses
into clothes that always looked more like costumes than children's wear.

The woman clicked away and then thanked your Grand
Mar, who did not give out her phone number because she knew
that as soon as the photos were developed she'd be hounded to
buy the box and album sets. To her surprise, when she returned

to End Point two weeks later, my face was smiling down at her from the window of the newly opened photo studio Lil' Shooting Stars.

When your Grand Par returned home from J & R Mechanics that afternoon, your Grand Mar demanded that he load our camera with her hoarded roll of Kodak film – "not the cheap Fuji film you always get" – and come take a look.

"Aww," growled your Grand Par, "just go yerself."

But he drove us to End Point in his Datsun. Grand Mar proudly pointed at the blown-up photo in the window.

"There," she said, tugging at his camera, "take it now."

"Don't be cheap," he said to her. "Besides, the glare from the glass is going to wreck everything and all you'll see is the reflection of Safeway." There was no way your Grand Par was going to stand in front of a hundred passing shoppers and take a photo of a photo in a window.

He went into the studio and came out ten minutes later with a receipt for a fifteen-dollar deposit, ten per cent of the purchase price. Even though he didn't give a stuff about Shooting Stars shopping-mall glory, he thought I was worth a hundred and fifty bucks, your Grand Par. He got the massive picture framed and hung it on our living-room wall, right above the television, even though your Grand Mar wanted to keep it in its box – she complained sunlight would fade it.

My duplicate self, my more famous twin, gazed out of the studio window for about six months. Our copy stayed on our living-room wall for years, until the day your Grand Mar yanked it down, telling your Grand Par that she'd made me, therefore it was hers.

"You already got the girl, can't you leave me with something to remember her by?" he shouted, but even though he called her terrible names, he didn't fight too hard. That was the trouble with your Grand Par, he was too placid. He thought it was easier to let your Grand Mar have her way.

Most of the time, your Grand Par had his head stuck in the bonnet or boot of a car, or sometimes slid under its metal belly. He used to let me go to work with him, pass him the tools. Ratchet. Ratchet extender. Nut splitter. Pliers. One time I got a smear of grease on the side of my nose, and he laughed and smeared the other side, then added another few lines down both my cheeks. "My tool kitty," he called me, and ruffled my hair, but not in the same way as your Grand Mar's lady customers, who stroked stroked stroked with their creeping fingers. Your Grand Par didn't think I needed cottonwool padding because he didn't think I could be marred, not even by engine grease.

Sometimes your Grand Par would take me on trips to pick up car parts from some of his friends who also owned home garages. They let me sit in the raised chassis of the vehicles they were fixing while they talked. Once his mate Steve even gave me a sip of his beer.

"Don't do that," your Grand Par protested. "You'll get her hooked on the stuff!" But he just laughed when I spat it right back out. "And lock up your sons in ten years' time. I don't want them near my Tool Kitty."

"You know, I used to have the biggest thing for Suzie Wong," Steve sighed.

"Who?"

"Don't tell me you've never heard of Suzie Wong. In that William Holden movie, about the gorgeous hooker."

"What's a hooker?" I asked.

"Never you mind," your Grand Par said to me. Then to Steve, "Don't talk about shit like that in front of my daughter."

Your Grand Par always had dirty hands, but I didn't mind them like your Grand Mar did. As a kid, I never let go of his hand when we crossed roads. But your Grand Mar, she would hold mine in hers like it was a bird she was trying to choke the life out of, and she would drag me, and the more she did this the more I scraped my heels against the footpath.

When I turned seven, she promised me a wonderful surprise, something so great we had to keep it a secret from your Grand Par, so we caught the bus into town instead of asking him for a lift. For once, I thought, she was going to take me somewhere really fun, like the roller rink or Wobbies World. We stopped at the chemist and I thought she was just running an errand before our adventure, until the lady behind the counter smiled at me and pointed to a revolving stand of tiny silver earrings.

I kicked and cried while they held my head still. "Don't be so ungrateful," your Grand Mar warned, but I had not signed up for guns and needles on my birthday.

It was days before your Grand Par noticed. I was outside standing on a stool, hanging out clothes on the line when the sun must have made the hoops wink. "Hey, Tool Kitty, what's that on your ear?"

That evening when they thought I was asleep, I could hear him yelling in their bedroom. "Why the hell would you do that? She's just a kid!"

She told him that in the Philippines, every girl had their ears pierced as a toddler: "If you let me do for her when she baby, then you will not be complain now."

"You're crazy. We don't do backwards shit like this in Australia."

"Yes, you Aussie think everything is child abuse."

The next year, your Grand Par wanted me to have a proper birthday party. "After the crap you put her through last year," he declared to your Grand Mar.

But there was no way she was going to let a herd of eight-year-olds rampage through her house. "They run crazy in my sunroom, use all my make-up brush like toys and wreck my business!"

"She can have it at Macca's, like her mate Danielle did a few weeks ago."

"Waste money."

"For Chrissake woman, and piercing her ears wasn't?"

By now the holes had closed over because I kept taking out the hoops.

In the end, your Grand Mar agreed to have a party at home, if I only had three friends over and we confined ourselves to the lounge room. The day before, she bought all the ingredients to make fried rice and spring rolls.

"What about a cake, Mah?" I asked, but the look she gave me made me shrink back through the doorway.

"Creating so much work for me!" she shouted, making it clear that no child ever had parties when she was growing up.

"What's wrong, Tool Kitty?" your Grand Par asked when he saw me sniffling in his garage.

When I told him, he drove me to Sims Tuckerbag and we bought sausage rolls and party pies, little foil hats and lollies, an ice-cream cake and candles. Your Grand Mar didn't say anything while she unpacked these treats.

At the party, Laura, Danielle and Tabitha stood awkwardly at the front door with their parents.

"Come in!" gushed your Grand Mar. "Have some food. I make so much!" She loaded up paper plates with spring rolls for the departing adults as I led my friends into the lounge room.

After the parents were gone, your Grand Mar came in and slammed two platefuls of party pies and sausage rolls down on the table. Then she walked out without saying a word.

Laura and Danielle looked at each other. "What's up with your mum?"

"I don't know."

"So . . . what are we supposed to do now?" Tabitha asked. Parents were supposed to organise activities. Laura's mum the Avon Lady had let us test different sample fruity lip-glosses and hand creams. Rebecca's dad had made an Astro Boy rocket with her and filled it with Wizz Fizzes. Both my parents had nicked off, but not together. They hadn't spoken in three days.

"Wait a sec, I'll ask my dad." I walked outside and into his garage. He was hunched over the hood of a car.

"Hey, Dad, aren't you coming in?"

"Nah, love, I'm a bit busy today. You girls want to do your girly things without this grimy old man in your way."

"But there's nothing to do."

"Didn't your mum leave a video out for you?"

She had, but it was our old pirated video cassette of Disney's *Snow White*, which I'd carefully hidden behind the television cabinet before my friends arrived.

"Love, I'll tell you what," your Grand Par said, "come get me when it's time for cake, okay?"

When I returned, none of the food had been touched, not even the lollies.

"Let's go outside," I suggested, hoping that if we loitered around the backyard long enough, your Grand Par would notice.

"Dad, we're bored," I finally told him.

He straightened up, eyeing off each of my friends. "Orright then. Not sure your friends are dressed for this special mission, but." He looked at me. "Neither are you. Never mind." We were all in bubble skirts, leggings and sweaters. He rifled through a drawer in the garage and showed us a bag.

"Cool! Water balloons!" declared Tabitha.

Laura looked anxious. "But we don't have any spare clothes."

"Don't worry, you can borrow Karuna's. Karuna, go inside and get some towels and old tracksuits of yours. Your friends can change in the loo."

"What are you doing with those?" your Grand Mar demanded, spotting me with my armload of clothes. I ignored her and ran outside.

Your Grand Par showed us how to fill the balloons with the garden hose and how to tie them, but he didn't need to show us how to throw them. Then he went back to his work while we squealed and hooted and splashed around the yard.

"You'd better not get my laundry wet!" your Grand Mar

yelled from the kitchen window. "You'd better bring in the laundry now!"

So I had to pause the game while we took the laundry off the line. I brought the basket of clothes inside and slammed it on the kitchen floor before running back out again.

When all our balloons had run out, your Grand Par set an old ceramic pot down one end of our driveway. He'd drawn a happy face on it with a permanent marker. "Girls, this is a pot of gold. It's got lollies and all kinds of goodies like that in it."

At the other end of the driveway, we stood drenched and giddy. Next he gave us a container of spanners and wrenches. "Piñatas are for wimps. Are youse wimps?"

"Nooooo!" we shouted back.

"This game is called Knock Its Block Off. You go first, Karuna. Show them how it's done."

I chucked my spanner as hard as I could. It made a loud clatter against the garage door. We all took our turns.

"Oh, crap!" Tabitha had thrown her spanner too wide and it smashed into the small Buddhist shrine your Grand Mar had set up against the side of the garage. Because your Grand Par would not allow her to have her false idols in the house, your Grand Mar had to keep her gods outdoors: a fierce, red-faced, black-bearded, sword-wielding god and a white, bored-looking goddess standing atop a lotus flower. Tabitha had knocked over the incense urn in front of the porcelain duo, sending their offerings of oranges rolling down the driveway.

Immediately, I checked for a reaction from the kitchen window, but your Grand Mar was no longer there. Phew.

"Don't worry, love, I'll sweep that up later," your Grand

Par said. "Cake time!" He went inside and brought out the ice-cream cake and a box of wafer cones. We heaped on massive mounds, the equivalent of shop-sized double and triple scoops. Your Grand Par just chortled. "Such greedy guts."

Your Grand Mar didn't make an appearance at all, until we heard the shouting inside the house. "Hah, thinks he's so clever, thinks he can put on a girl's birthday party. Mud and grass all over the bathroom floor, extra towels to wash, and they won't even remember to give the clothes back!" No one could understand her except me, but we could all hear her banging dishes around in the kitchen. "See who helps me clean up?"

"You and your mates better come with me to the garage, Tool Kitty," your Grand Par warned. "She's in one of her states again." He winked at me. "I have a surprise for you in there."

The girls crowded around the two big boxes he handed to me. "You got roller skates!" exclaimed Tabitha. She picked up my new helmet and tried it on. "This is so cool."

Your Grand Mar never let me use the roller skates, of course. "Do you want to break your neck?" she asked. "Why do you think he loves you when he's trying to get you killed?"

But that afternoon, your Grand Par's party confirmed my long-held convictions: your Grand Par was the best; your Grand Mar was the worst. I just hoped my friends hadn't heard her out in the driveway, sweeping up the pieces of her shrine, cursing and crying.

We had a brick house back then, the insides looking and smelling like the pastel colours of Neapolitan ice-cream, with a room that opened out to the backyard through sliding glass doors. Your Grand Mar called it a sunroom because there was a sky-light. She had a sink installed, and bought a plastic-covered mauve reclining chair for a hundred and seventeen dollars. That's where she conducted her business. With a grey pencil and three shades of skin-tint she could conjure up double-fold eyelids where there had been none. With blush and some brown powder she could define a jawline, and her speciality – the thing that had brides-to-be driving across town – was that she would spend an hour and a half gluing small clusters of silk eyelashes onto their eyelids. "This is the newest technique from Japan," she would say. "None of the local businesses do it yet."

I lay on that reclining chair while she twiddled with my lashes, perfecting her technique. It would have been a different experience if we were a different mother and daughter, because beauty treatments are meant to be bonding and relaxing, but for me, going to the dentist would have been better. Every part of my body would tense. Every hole in me would clench tight like a fist.

"Don't scrunch your eyes like that," scolded your Grand Mar. "I can't attach the glue properly! And you'll get wrinkles."

"I hate lying here like a dead body."

"Be quiet, I can't concentrate when you open your mouth."

"Why can't you just get one of those stupid plastic hairdress-ing heads to practise on?"

"Do you know how much those heads cost?" she retorted. "And they're hopeless. Working on them would be too easy. They don't blink or fidget or screw their eyes. They don't talk back."

When she was done and I opened my heavy-feathered eye-lids, I saw the world through a half-black shadow. I looked like one of those sad, long-lashed cow puppets on *Sesame Street*. This lasted for two weeks, until the fake lashes dropped off, along with my real ones. What a relief to see the world again without the top third blacked out.

Because your Grand Mar never learned to drive, she sent your Grand Par on errands, and sometimes I tagged along. He didn't care what I wore. "She's fine the way she is!" he'd grumble, when your Grand Mar tried to force me to change out of my tracksuit into a frock. "Leave her alone, for Chrissake. We're just going to your friggin' make-up supplier."

"I don't want Thanh see my daughter dress like a beggar."

"She's dressed like a normal kid! Bugger off, woman."

And I'd clamber into the car before she could grab me. As he drove off, your Grand Par chuckled. "You cheeky monkey."

The suppliers mostly conducted their businesses from cardboard boxes in their homes. When Thanh opened the door, I wasn't sure she was even going to let us in, because usually your Grand Mar picked up the lipsticks and powders while your Grand Par waited in the car with the radio on.

"Mr Kelly, hello. Your wife tell me you come," she chimed cheerfully. "Business must be good. She tell me she got two bride today." Thanh's long pink nails beckoned us into her sitting room, where your Grand Par perched on the edge of a paisley velour sofa. Opening up a cardboard box, Thanh showed us the contents. "I have her order here. Total of seventeen thirty-two."

Your Grand Par put down twenty dollars. "Don't worry about the change, love. Keep it."

Your Grand Mar would never have done that. She also would have carefully checked to make sure that the lipsticks were all sealed and that no blush powders had cracked.

"Wait!" said Thanh, disappearing down the hallway. She came back with something lolly-coloured and glittery in a see-through case for me. I wasn't sure whether it was for my cheeks, nails or lips and didn't want it, but took it out of politeness. All the times I'd visited with your Grand Mar, Thanh had just ignored me. "You better keep a careful eye on her when she get big," she told your Grand Par.

"If she turns out as pretty as you." He winked at her.

When I was very young, I loved the attention of adults. I didn't have to do anything, I just had to let your Grand Mar spiff me up. A real doll, people used to say. In fact, the less I said, the more endearing they seemed to find me. Your Grand Mar's customers would pinch the top of my nose. "This one won't need contouring make-up for her wedding!" They would stare at my eyes and say, "Girls have surgery just to have this one's eyelids." "Those back home use special creams just to have the skin tone this one has." I'd seen what my "back home" brown-skinned, jabby-elbowed cousins looked like. In all the photos in my mother's albums, they wore the same yellow or green smocked dresses, too short to hide their scaly knees.

"This one is so lucky," the customers would say about me, and after a while, in my mind This One became These Two. There were two of me: the outside one, who was pinched and patted and petted, and the inside me, who felt contempt for these women's pawing hands, their looks like little hooks. They gave me a power that I didn't want or need, but which I secretly liked.

And then all too soon, I found out how quickly it could dissolve.

I started to get freckles. They appeared on my arms, legs, nose, like I'd got in the way of some reckless god stomping in a muddy puddle. "You were such a white baby," your Grand Mar sighed. "Who would have thought that you could end up blotchy?" She told me to stay out of the sun and bought me bottles of Oil of Ulan and Banana Boat sunscreen, wide-brimmed hats and even a little plastic Hello Kitty umbrella for sunny days, which I refused to carry.

It started with those freckles, and then it was my teeth – the two middle ones were too large and rabbity, the canines too sharp – then my height, and then my oily face. Soon there seemed to be nothing left of miniature me, the me on whom your Grand Mar had pinned all her hopes. She never embraced me when I came of age. Her way of showing me love was pestering your Grand Par to put his money where my mouth was and get me braces. Then it was no more playing ball, even by myself against the wall.

"If that ball whacks you in the mouth it could rip all your teeth out, since they're connected like a zipper," warned your Grand Mar. "One thousand dollars, knocked off, just like that!"

She was pissed off because my beauty didn't come naturally anymore, and I was reminded of this every day when I looked at our living-room wall and saw the most perfect self I would ever be, *a self I didn't even remember being*, smiling down at me like a twinkle-star on top of a Christmas tree with no presents underneath.

Chapter 2

Your Grand Mar's approach to fashion was unfortunately exactly the same as her make-up technique, but what worked wonders for the face did not transfer onto the body, especially not a body going into high school. I knew your Grand Mar didn't do colours the right way, like Punky Brewster did with her different-coloured socks, or Cyndi Lauper with her different-coloured hair. All your Grand Mar's colours had to match or line up in some way, darkening as they descended, like a full-body sunset: pink scrunchie, red fleecy jumper, brown skirt, grey tights, black shoes.

A week before I started Year Nine, she wanted to take me to Kmart to buy stationery, but I refused to wear the white jumper she'd bought me, with its enormous red-sequinned lips appliquéd on the chest and matching sequinned headband. I didn't want to look like cheap advertising for her services. "You used to be such a good child," she sighed. By good she meant obedient.

That was the summer I turned fourteen and met Tweezer. Her real name was Teresa Christianna Zafeiriou, but the way your Grand Mar pronounced it, her first name clamped down tight and wouldn't loosen, and because she adored your Grand Mar, Tweezer let it stand.

Tweezer sat next to me in our first homeroom at Christ Our Saviour College, and the first thing I noticed were her tiny wrists, like twigs I could snap without much effort. She had worried eyes behind round glasses, reminding me of brown marbles rolling in green cups. There was not a single part of her that could keep still. Unlike the tasteful silver crosses some girls wore around their necks – sometimes with a tiny cubic zirconia in the centre – Tweezer was wearing a massive heavy antique gold crucifix on a thick chain. Worse, she had it hanging outside of her blouse and jumper. It was ugly as sin.

"Someone's prepared for the second coming," muttered Deanna, sitting behind us.

When Tweezer realised that Deanna was talking about her, she hunched over and looked down at her desk, too self-conscious even to tuck the crucifix in.

"Come on, put that away," I said to her.

She still wouldn't look at me, but her right hand moved to cup the cross.

"You think that when Jesus returns," I whispered, "he will like a billion people flashing that at him?"

She looked at me, confused, panicked.

"Let me put it this way. If I got killed by a lightsaber, I wouldn't want to come back to Earth and find a billion people flashing bloody lightsabers at me."

I saw the sideways curve of a smile creep onto her face. She tucked it, and the crucifix, away.

When homeroom was over and we stood up to go to our next class, Mrs Morello tapped Tweezer on the shoulder. "Karuna will look after you," she said, mistaking my height for maturity.

That first week, I walked Tweezer to class and sat with her at recess and lunch. I wasn't an outcast at school, just one of those girls who moved from group to group. Other girls tolerated me fine, some even liked me, but never enough to latch on as a best friend. I was just a colourful extra in the dozens of independent little sitcoms that happened every week on the concrete lawns.

Poor Tweezer – I'd never met a soul more grateful for my company. Sometimes I even caught her staring at me in awe. Admittedly, I liked the attention. Tweezer genuinely thought I could be really popular if I just tried harder, and she would make half-hearted attempts to convince me of this. "Jamilla is pretty," she would comment, "but I think it's just because of her haircut. You're way more beautiful. And you're funny, too. You could have so many more friends if you took the time to really work on one group."

This is why I liked Tweezer so much. She saw me as classier than I was, and she cared that I should have more friends. She kept devising strategies for my social climb, with a child's trust that I would not abandon her when I reached the top. Maybe deep down she knew her plans would never really work; maybe she knew I didn't care enough about fitting in.

Or maybe it was just that Tweezer hadn't been at Christ Our Saviour for that long. Neither Tweezer nor your Grand Mar realised that I was like a dusty, back-of-the-shelf version of a white girl, one of those dusky Barbies that gets shoved in the discount pile; and among the Asian girls at school I was a dumb-arse giantess. Those girls cooed over my chocolate hair and light lion eyes, but I knew they didn't take my smarts seriously. I looked nice but no one really wanted me.

Tweezer had this obsession with princesses. Not real princesses like Diana, but Disney princesses. She was way too old for stuff like that, but she didn't know it. She once told me she would name her firstborn Aurora, after Sleeping Beauty.

"What if it's a boy?" I asked.

"It won't be a boy," she said, with deep certainty. Boys – like her younger brother Spiros, like the ones who went to St Andrew's Catholic College – didn't exist for Tweezer. Men either, unless they were princes.

Which is why Tweezer got it into her head that she really wanted to see the new movie *Labyrinth*. The poster of the princess in the white dress had sucked her in. It didn't seem like my kind of film, but I wasn't going to miss out. We told our parents we wanted to see a film about fairies, hoping they'd let us go by ourselves. It was the first time Tweezer and I had met up outside school. I got the sense that it was a big deal for her, that she might not have been to the movies before.

But then your Grand Mar insisted on tagging along. "Two beautiful young girls walking around by yourself," she told Tweezer after school. "What if the boys don't leave you alone?"

Your Grand Mar had no idea about the boys who hung around the arcade playing Metroid, more interested in seeing Samus Aran in an electronic bikini than in the two of us. Tweezer just giggled. It was likely that not many people had told her she was beautiful before, so she didn't mind your Grand Mar being there.

We arrived at End Point early, so we could go to Safeway to get our lollies and one litre of chocolate milk, because, according to your Grand Mar, getting treats in the cinema was "daytime robbery". She had also brought along paper cups.

I waited for Tweezer, noticing that Lil' Shooting Stars had been replaced by a store that printed people's photos on T-shirts.

Tweezer's father arrived with her. An unsmiling man with a moustache, he took one long look at your Grand Mar, then at me, and then asked Tweezer something I couldn't understand.

"No, she's Australian," Tweezer replied.

He shot off more rapid-fire words at her.

"My dad wants me waiting here, immediately after the movie ends," she said to me, "so he can pick me up when he finishes his delivery work."

"I take her to our house and you pick her up," your Grand Mar told him. "Is safer. I come with the girls to see movie."

Tweezer translated, and I could see the look change on her father's face. Like dough in an oven, he warmed and softened. Obviously he approved of your Grand Mar chaperoning us.

He pulled a small spiral notebook out of his trouser pocket and handed it to her. "Address, please."

After your Grand Mar wrote it down in the careful, letter-by-letter way of the illiterate, he studied it for a while and nodded. Then he left.

In the cinema, Tweezer sat on my left and your Grand Mar on my right. When the lights dimmed, I expected to see gothic Muppets, like in *The Dark Crystal*. But this was something else.

From the moment Jareth the Goblin King appeared on the screen, I was transfixed.

Afterwards, I couldn't stop thinking about the King in his motorcycle jacket and ballet tights. He was both Peter Pan and James Dean, but very, very old. Everything I felt that summer of my fourteenth year suddenly had a gravitational pull, and he was it – the molten centre. I'd desired things before – toys, a Cabbage Patch doll, a silver lamé jacket – but now I realised that people could desire *each other*, that it wasn't the same at all as desiring an object, and it was different again from wanting the love of a parent or a friend or even a boyfriend.

No, this was something I couldn't control, because if I could have chosen, I would not have chosen David Bowie. I would have chosen one of the Rickys from New Edition or Menudo. Those guys were boyfriend material, as *Dolly* magazine told us. They were like different models of reliable new vehicles – Ford Taurus, Honda Accord, Toyota LandCruiser. Then there was Jareth. A jaguar. Not the car, either. Something fast and dangerous and sleek, made of skin and sound. Something that can want you back.

"So lame," sighed Tweezer. "So weird. There wasn't even a prince in the end, it was just that creepy goblin with the grey teeth who wanted to make her his slave. Gross."

"So creepy," I muttered, burning with shame. It was embarrassing to feel this way about a deep-voiced man who wore make-up and lavender stockings. Maybe your Grand Mar and her brides had altered me in some way, tweaked my preferences. I wondered if your Grand Mar could sense anything. She'd sat expressionless through the whole movie.

Outside, these dark, pestering thoughts couldn't fester. The sky was metallic blue-white, reflecting off the automatic doors of End Point's west entrance.

We caught the bus back to our place. When Tweezer saw your Grand Mar's sunroom, she stood there, gawking. One of those polite guests who wouldn't sit down unless you invited her to, Tweezer stayed put like Audrey Hepburn outside Tiffany's until I led her inside. Never had I considered what this room might look like to someone who loved the idea of romance so much, with its big windows, lace curtains and the dresses left by brides on hangers like swooning ghosts.

"Wow," Tweezer breathed, and I knew that this more than made up for the movie.

I could tell her fingers were itching to touch everything, so I let her open one of your Grand Mar's make-up cases. I told her she could look through the magazines on the coffee table, and even lie on the sunbed, so she did, very cautiously. Soon, Tweezer was even game enough to pick up one of your Grand Mar's blue fake-leather albums of the before-and-after brides.

"Amazing," she said, poring over every page. "So this is what your mum does."

Honestly, I preferred the "before" photos of the women. The "after" shots all had the same haughty "I know I'm beautiful" look. Before a full make-up and hair service, you could see in each woman's eyes how scared she was that she wouldn't be the Cinderella, but the one whose plainness no amount of powder could change.

"Hey, what's this?" Tweezer asked, pulling out a slimmer album from the bottom of the pile. The red album. God no. I knew how wrong the images inside looked: me, from ten to fourteen, in full make-up, wearing the wedding dresses from the sunroom, the extra yardage carefully pinned back with pegs.

Every time your Grand Mar wanted to try a new look or technique, she'd practise on me. The first time she'd told me to wear a bride's gown, I'd said, "No, we aren't allowed!"

"Nonsense," she'd replied, "as long as we don't get any make-up on it, it'll be fine. You're so tiny it's not like you'll stretch it. And you'll only have it on for less than a minute while I take the picture. They won't even notice."

Tweezer stared at a photo of me in a dress with a tapered waist and sleeves like tulle parachutes, and I remembered how Jennifer Connelly's head rose above the silver cloud surrounding her shoulders, searching for her baby brother but, really, craning to see mean-faced Bowie, and how he looked at her as if he wanted to eat her.

Your Grand Mar came in and saw what Tweezer was looking at. "My daughter, she look like Book Shield?"

I looked nothing like Brooke Shields. For starters, I was the wrong colour. But Tweezer just nodded and smiled.

After that day, Tweezer loved coming over to our place, because she was one of those girls whose fathers would belt the back of her legs full of welts if she so much as put a smear of Vaseline on her lips. The closest she'd ever come to applying make-up was licking a Jaffa and using it as lipstick and blush. Your Grand Mar didn't mind Tweezer either, even let her sit and watch while she worked on customers' faces. I couldn't have thought of anything more boring, but Tweezer was so excited she'd sit on her hands to keep them still.

I suppose Tweezer admired your Grand Mar because she was everything her own mum wasn't – your Grand Mar's words could create cavities, the way she spread compliments like jam on toast, right up to the edges. "But she's such a fake," I said over and over to Tweezer. "She backstabs her customers when they leave. You should hear the things she says to me while she's smiling at them."

"Look at this one's pimples," your Grand Mar would tell me in our dialect. "A face like a leftover plate of fried rice. They always have worse skin than us. It might be whiter but it crumples faster. And she thinks that an eyebrow tweeze will fix everything!" But to the customer: "What beautiful eyelash you have. So long. So curl."

"At least your mother can be nice in public. Mine can't even do that," said Tweezer. It was true – Tweezer's mother was charmless, severe, already like a wilted grandma. But there was something about her I admired: she was not a fake. She didn't know how to be. She had a job standing in a plastic apron in the early hours of the morning scraping the barbs off roses on an assembly line.

Tweezer's mum had filled their house with prints of cracked mosaic saints with their eyes rolled towards the heavens, as if they were in their death throes and on the verge of seeing the only thing that could put them back together again. A framed picture of a holy man Tweezer called Archbishop Stylianos was the only photograph in the living room. The furniture was too big for their small room, and they must have been to at least thirty weddings because their cabinet was filled with little organza bags of pastel almonds all at different shades of fade. And of course, it smelt of roses, because Mrs Zafeiriou took the imperfect ones home.

At first, Tweezer's mother, like her father, mistook me for another Greek girl. "Same colour," she said. "Look this girl. One us." But I had one of those faces that could have been anything. She used to kiss me on both cheeks, because I was tall and dumb and had a sweet smile; such bumbling charm could never corrupt her daughter.

In her room, Tweezer had three Barbies. Like me, she was never allowed the Ken doll. Unlike me, she still kept her Barbies in their boxes, displayed neatly in a row on her shelf. Your Grand Mar had bought me Barbies as a kid, thinking that I could make frocks for them out of her fabric offcuts, not that I would peel their clothes off and tetris their limbs together. The day she found my entwined Barbies, she gave me a look far dirtier than what my dolls were doing.

Back when I was seven, I found an empty matchbox in the street with a photo of a white marble sculpture on it. The sculpture was of two people, a man and a woman, linked by their arms and one leg, faces kissing. I'd never seen anything so beautiful, but I also knew instinctively that it was *wrong*. I secretly wrapped it in a tissue, a blanket to keep my two naked friends warm. When she discovered it under my bed, your Grand Mar yelled at me for keeping something so filthy. "A girl is like this tissue," she warned me. "Once dirtied, she can never be clean again."

Then she tossed the matchbox in the bin, among the eggshells and vacuum cleaner fluff. Later, when she wasn't looking, I retrieved it, wiped it clean and hid it between the cupboard and the wall. Sometimes, when I was alone, I would take it out and examine it for a long time. At the bottom left corner, printed in tiny cursive letters, was *A Rodin*. From then on, I thought that a *rodin* was something sexy and forbidden, in the same way I thought lingerie was pronounced *linger-ree*.

And still, I believed I was infinitely more worldly than Tweezer. Although she shared everything she did or thought with me, I didn't share certain thoughts with her, like the secret matchbox I had once kept. And only I knew the truth about your Grand Mar's controlling ways.

"Tread carefully," she would tell me. "A girl who makes one wrong move is wrecked for life." She was full of such gems. But by fourteen I knew that I was separate from her, that she could no longer look at my face and find out what I was thinking, like she could when I was a kid.

Chapter 3

didn't blame your Grand Par for leaving. Your Grand Mar had kept pestering him the same way she pestered me. "Why you go out with Steve and Dragan so much?" "Why buy her that Etchy Sketch? She can use paper and pen." "What's this alo-minimum foil? Do we really need?"

She had even begrudged him his daily newspaper. "Why you buy this newspaper when we get one free every week in our letterbox?"

"That's the local paper," he explained. "This is the national one. A man's gotta keep himself informed."

"Why don't you watch news on television instead?" It was not a suggestion, it was an accusation, and he was sick of those.

"For God's sake, lay off me, woman!" your Grand Par roared.

"I just trying to do best for this family," your Grand Mar would sulk. "Some wives don't care and just let your money go go go, they just spend spend spend all."

She told him off for buying me Hungry Jack's when he picked me up after school because she didn't want me to get fat, for letting me help out in the garage when I was needed in the house, and for cutting my fringe one day because I'd asked him to.

Your Grand Par was also probably sick of the bickering that

went on between your Grand Mar and me. He was a man who made up for his lack of words with his ability to get vehicles humming again. There were always at least four cars around our house – three parked in our garage and driveway that your Grand Par was working on, and one at the kerb, out of which tumbled a soon-to-be wife ready for her makeover session, often in coloured tights and a button-down shirt.

Your Grand Par didn't like people who thought too highly of themselves. If a customer was being precious with their Volvo 240, he'd mutter, "So grandular," which I wasn't sure was a word.

"It'll be good fer her," your Grand Par said to your Grand Mar when he stopped paying for my Catholic education. "Not being taught by those nuns, clinging to that pretty little wog girl who's shit-scared of her own shadow. A state education is a fine education, stop being so grandular."

"Your dad no longer wants to pay for you to be protected," your Grand Mar said, like he'd been shelling out for my sanitary products or a personal bodyguard. "He won't keep you in that safe school anymore." That school wedged between a convent and a biscuit factory, purity and sweetness on either side, where my best friend Tweezer still dreamed about Ken-doll princes.

"Look after yourself," your Grand Par said to me before he left. He didn't mean take care of my nails; he meant don't get hit by a car or break any limbs or let boys take advantage of me. "My Tool Kitty."

Once the divorce was a done deal, all your Grand Mar's Asian brides disappeared. "No one wants their wedding make-up done by a divorced woman," those ex-customers said. The ones who had once happily paid good money, the ones who had been eager to book her five months in advance because she had been so popular, were the same ones now so considerately warning their friends against tempting fate: "What terrible luck that would bring." There just wasn't enough interest from Anglo customers for your Grand Mar to keep going, so she didn't.

So that's how we ended up moving to the commission flats. They rose twenty storeys high, stacked like brown slab cakes. Inside, our kitchen had a black and white lino floor and wooden cabinets painted pale green. Except for the murky carpet in the bedrooms and the small windows, I didn't think the place was too bad. But the day we moved in, your Grand Mar made a huge fuss of sterilising everything with a ten-litre plastic container of diluted White King bleach. "Who knows what grots were here before us?" she complained. "Who knows what germs they left behind?"

Because your Grand Mar was so miserable, I did what she wanted: squatting and scrubbing the gaps between the tiles on the bathroom floor with an old toothbrush, digging in the shower-screen gaps with my fingers to get rid of the black mould. But on the phone, she told different aunties – those sisters she so resented in the Philippines – that I was lazy and didn't do any work and how she wished I was like my cousins. She said that halfies were idle, that I got it from my father. That was the day I missed your Grand Par the most.

The flat had two bedrooms, but your Grand Mar piled all our unopened boxes in the smaller one and left my single bed disassembled, leaning against the wall.

"What do you think you're doing?" she asked, when she saw me trying to pull the mattress down.

"Why did you leave all this crap in my room?" I protested. "I can't set up my bed."

"What do you mean, your room? You don't have your own room anymore. It's just the two of us now, we have to stick together. Besides, can't you see there's no space?"

Yeah, I thought, if you hadn't pilfered Dad's possessions, including instruction manuals for household appliances we no longer owned and jars of dried-up resin, we'd have plenty of space.

She believed that if I shared the bed with her, I would be delivered from evil because I would have no private spaces for bad thoughts to bloom like fungi.

"Karuna, you have to stay by me," she said on that first night in our new flat. "I have no one. I spent so long making others' ugly faces look good, but now not one of them will even look at mine."

I turned to the wall, my back curled away from her. She was so annoying. I just wanted to go to sleep. It had been a tiring day scrubbing and unpacking.

She'd bought me a pink cotton nightgown, on sale at Kmart. It had a Peter Pan collar made with eyelet lace and went half-way down my calves, and while she ranted I lay in bed like an unblinking, unthinking, crooked Copperart Victorian doll.

"Don't ignore me!" she said. "I've lost everything."

"You're not the only one," I muttered.

"You!" she accused. "What have you lost?"

Was she kidding? How selfish could one person be?

"You still have your mother!" She was always the victim, and couldn't see that her whingeing had driven your Grand Par nuts. But I didn't say anything.

"When I arrived in Australia, I cried at the airport," she told me. "He was so old! I hadn't expected him to be so old."

Oh no, I thought. Now I'd be awake for at least another forty minutes. I knew this story well, because she had it on loop like a broken single-track cassette. She would begin by telling me that your Grand Par had tricked her, sent a photo of himself with darker hair. "I should have known but back in the Old Country all the photos were yellow at the edges because of the cheap film-paper and the heat." She would mention the raisin of a woman standing next to him at the airport – his mother, clutching the string of blue pearls around her neck with one hand and your Grand Par with the other, as though his new wife was going to rob her.

After they married, they lived in a brown and yellow house, faded like the photograph. "The cupboards were painted the colour of when you eat too many mangoes and get the runs," your Grand Mar said, but she had never lived in a house with carpet before. She thought she'd reached the height of luxury, until the first summer when rancid grey-brown stains started to spread beneath the loops of wool in the corner of the lounge room, and your Grand Par discovered that a family of mice had met their end beneath the rotting floorboards.

When she arrived, like the Little Mermaid your Grand Mar had no voice, so people saw her only as your Grand Par's catch. In fact, many thought it was all very fishy: that good boy Ron, who should have married a sweet wholesome loaf like Mary from Moonee Ponds, ended up with a woman who looked as if she'd been washed up like flotsam and jetsam on the shore, all tangly black hair and wood-brown skin.

Grand Par's mother didn't bully her daughter-in-law into submission, as mothers-in-law from the Old Country would. "What are you doing?" she would ask your Grand Mar five times a day, even though it was clear that your Grand Mar was hanging out the clothes, or taking down the curtains to clean, or lining the cupboards with BI-LO advertisements. Your Grand Mar would reply "cleaning" or "wiping", and Grand Par's ma would just hover for a little longer before going inside to watch telly.

"That Ghost woman was not so terrible," sighed your Grand Mar. "She minded her own business, I minded mine. I was careful to learn how to cook food the way she liked it. Mind you, that wasn't too hard, since those Ghosts just boil everything to crap. When she died, I was even sad." She sighed again.

"Your father ruined everything for me. I left my country and family for him and his fake photo, and he left me alone in a foreign land to raise a child by myself!" This was her side of the story – her life had had momentum, respectability; it had been leading somewhere, and then, suddenly, it was over. "When you get married, choose carefully. Don't do it just to escape your parents."

She thought she knew everything, that her suffering had given her some sort of wisdom, when all it had done was make her bitter. As if I would choose marriage as an escape! That was just swapping one owner for another.

In the bed, I burned like a mosquito coil, hot and irritated.

"What do you think you're doing, turning away on purpose when I'm talking to you?" She poked my back with one finger.

"I'm just trying to sleep."

"Exactly the same as your father. He wouldn't listen to me either."

Shut up already, I thought.

"No one has ever listened to me. What I say has always been unimportant."

She got into my skin like a splinter and just kept digging in.

"I raised you. If it weren't for me, where would you be, huh? You've turned out to be useless! Now I have no one!"

She started to sniff. The weeping was the worst. I felt like a terrible daughter, because the louder she wailed and the longer she cried, the less sympathy I could muster. During the day she treated me like a dumb kid, and at night she expected me to be like a mum who would soothe her. But I had no idea how to fix something that she had broken herself.

Then your Grand Mar got a job, and finally I could hear my own thoughts again and get some proper sleep. She began working evenings at a restaurant called Siamese Please, a name that always reminded me of those horrible slanty-eyed, curtain-climbing cats in *Lady and the Tramp*. At Siamese Please, the carpets had been maroon but were now almost black. There was wood panelling on the walls, and above that, five rows of mirrored tiles. The waitresses were smiling Chinese and Vietnamese girls in Thai sarong-dresses.

Your Grand Mar was out the back on the woks, because she was too old to dazzle customers. Sometimes the sizzle of the wok sounded a lot like a tap turned on full blast. Now we always had take-away food in plastic containers in our fridge. Whenever I visited, the manager, a middle-aged woman named Aunt Yenny, who had eyebrows as sparse as the hair on a lady's fingers, asked me if I wanted fried ice-cream. "Ang moh girls always want ice-cream," she said to your Grand Mar.

I didn't like fried ice-cream, but I would dutifully eat up a bowl every time I was there. On the bus back, your Grand Mar would complain, "That bitch is trying to get you fat because she's jealous she doesn't have a daughter," which made absolutely no sense to me, but I supposed your Grand Mar was just angry about working for Aunt Yenny when she'd worked for herself for so long.

Aunt Yenny was from Timor, which, according to your Grand Mar's hierarchy of Chineseness, meant that she should have been beneath us, hailing from such an annexed, backwater land, whereas the Philippines was so sought after that two colonial powers had fought over it. Aunt Yenny's husband, Uncle Winsome, was the cook in the restaurant and he seemed like an Asian version of your Grand Par – a hardworking, wordless man who was always doing something useful with his hands.

Your Grand Mar now often arrived home around one in the morning. After she helped Aunt Yenny and Uncle Winsome close the restaurant, they'd give her a lift back and drop her at the bottom of our flats. If I stirred in our bed, she would rouse me and ask me to give her a back massage. The muscles on her back felt as tight as the meat of an overcooked supermarket chook.

*

Aunt Yenny invited us over to her house for a barbeque on Australia Day, when the restaurant was closed. *Beware of the Dogs*, said the sign at the front of her house, and we could hear loud barking from behind the gate. Turns out they had a German Shepherd and a Great Dane, and two droopy-shouldered boys cleaning the droppings from the grass with shovels and plastic bags.

"When I first arrived, I chose this name for myself," said Uncle Winsome, "because I thought I would be a millionaire by now. But how do they say it? You win some, you lose some!"

Uncle Winsome asked me what year I was in at school, and I told him.

"Oh, Year Eleven is a difficult year," said Aunt Yenny. "Too bad she's no longer at the Catholic school. Wayson and Wilson both go to St Andrew's. Less derelict than the local government school. No girls to distract them, either." One of Aunt Yenny's two quiet boys passed me the kecap manis sauce. Your Grand Mar smiled at him but her eyes glinted the opposite – for some reason, she had taken an intense dislike to Yenny's sons.

"You know," said Uncle Winsome, "if you are worried about her marks, some university students came by the restaurant the other day to ask if they could leave flyers for a free tutoring service. Remind me to give you one tomorrow night at work."

Before we left, Aunt Yenny said to your Grand Mar, "Here, let me pack you a box of barbequed meat. Your daughter is cute, but far too skinny."

We passed the *Beware of the Dogs* sign on our way out. "It's not those dogs you have to beware of," your Grand Mar muttered to me when we were outside the gate. "It's her human dogs inside."

More and more, I was getting unwanted attention when I was out. Once, a boy followed me halfway home from school. He was more a Dachshund puppy than a Doberman, though, and looked like he might cry when I turned around and yelled, "I know you're stalking me. What the hell?" Shame-faced, he just ran the other way. Sometimes a carload of teenagers from the local technical school would drive by, wind down their windows and wolf-whistle, but these were hunters in packs – when I walked right past a single boy on the way home from school, he wouldn't dare say a word.

Another time, an old man stopped his lawnmower as I walked by his house. He ambled to his front hedge and I thought he was going to badger me, but he just said, "You are the loveliest thing. Bless your heart."

Of course, I knew the difference between simple appreciation and complicated danger, the difference between the old lawn-mower man and the moving tin-can of hoons. There was a gap between the sudden intake of breath from joy and surprise, and turning asthmatic with lust. Some men minded the gap. Others did not see it. Still others saw it and disregarded it, like the trio of men in business suits outside the office building near the bus stop. I noticed them straightaway, because they were looking at me so silently. They didn't say a word to each other, thinking the looks and gestures they exchanged were in some coded, grown-up sign language: a bent eyebrow, a curled finger, a secret sneer. Then one of them came and sat very close to me. I was still in my school uniform, waiting for the bus that would take me to Siamese Please, and all I could think about was that nursery rhyme "Little Miss Muffet". *Along came a spider and sat down beside her.*

Luckily, the bus arrived right then and I jumped up. "See you later, sweetheart," the man called out as I stepped onto the bus, so that the passengers would think I had such a caring and respectable dad.

I never told your Grand Mar about any of these incidents. I had a feeling she'd blame me somehow, or try to take even more of my freedom.

A few weeks after working at Siamese Please, your Grand Mar got sick. It might have been the exhaustion, or the heat of the cooking room, but one Friday morning she returned burning with a fever.

"Help me, Karuna," she said, prodding me in the ribs and turning on the bedside lamp. "I feel terrible."

"Do we have Panadol?" I asked.

"No, I don't take that crap," she said. "It doesn't work." She waved a porcelain spoon at me, and a jar of Tiger Balm oil. "I need to you to scrape my back to release the heat."

After peeling off her jumper and shirt, she lay on the blanket, chest down.

I sat up. "What am I supposed to do with this spoon?"

"Scrape it across my back in long lines. From shoulder to waist, down each side of my spine. It will release the heat."

She'd already rubbed Tiger Balm oil thickly on the spoon – the stinging-mint scent was powerful. I did as I was told. "Harder," she instructed, so I scraped harder. Suddenly, tiny red dots appeared where the spoon had been, in a thick line down the side of her spine.

"Mum, you're bleeding!" I cried.

"Don't stop now, it's working," your Grand Mar commanded. "That's just the fever coming out." Instead of looking tortured, she actually relaxed, shoulders sinking into the pillows with relief.

"This is what I used to do for my own mother," she told me. "She used to sell coconut pandan cakes at the marketplace. When she got sick, she'd ask me to scrape her back with a coin like you're doing now."

When I'd scraped her whole back and she looked like she'd had a terrible flogging, your Grand Mar exhaled, a loud, contented groan. Then she fell fast asleep where she lay, still on her stomach.

Chapter 4

Remember how Yenny's husband said that there was free tutoring at the government house?" Every public building was a government house to your Grand Mar. "You should go and get yourself prepared for your new school. They might put you in a class away from the druggies and sluts if they find out you are clever."

Your Grand Mar didn't really care about my academic results. She'd always been more interested in what was hanging off my ears than what was between them. She just wanted me kept under surveillance. She had found herself another job, a day job, three blocks away from Siamese Please. She'd been picking up some coat hangers at the Yen Huot variety store when she saw a sign in the window next door: *Salon asissant wanted. Inquiry in.* She went in but the owner wouldn't give her the time of day, wouldn't even look at her once she realised your Grand Mar was not a paying customer but a too-old, unskilled Asian who couldn't speak proper English.

Your Grand Mar showed up the next day with her albums. Without a word she set them on the glass counter near the cash register, and when there was a lull in the customers, she held them up for the owner, Mrs Osman, to look at.

She got herself a job eyebrow tweezing and waxing, and within a few weeks she was blow-drying hair and doing simple trims. She was good, your Grand Mar.

She got paid a paper fistful of money every week. She'd leave early in the morning for one job, and wouldn't be back from the other job until past eleven at night. I knew your Grand Mar didn't trust me to be at home by myself. She wasn't sure where I'd go, or who I'd go with. Sometimes she looked at me like I was a spoiled brat, and other times like I was the worst bits of your Grand Par blended into one person.

When your Grand Par was around I used to hang out in his garage, but now I would be in that stinking-hot flat lining the drawers with cut-up cornflakes boxes, or doing other depressing busywork your Grand Mar devised to keep me out of trouble. She never gave me any money, so I couldn't even catch a bus to see Tweezer; and Tweezer was so closely monitored there was no way she could catch a cold by herself, let alone public transport to see me.

I probably didn't need tutoring. I had been doing okay at school the last year, and could figure most things out by myself – if not one hundred per cent then perhaps eighty per cent, which was good enough for me. That summer after your Grand Par left, so many hours crawled by snail-like, leaving behind moist trails of dire, idle time. Finally I decided I needed to go out, just to make something, anything, happen.

So one morning I pulled on my jeans and chucked on one of your Grand Par's short-sleeved flannels. I wound my hair in a knot and whacked on one of his caps, the one with *TOYO TYRES* on the front. If your Grand Mar were home, she would have made me dress up even for this. She still expected me to wear a plaid miniskirt or a dress with two cotton strawberries for pockets. Instead, I had begun to raid their wardrobe, the side where your Grand Par's clothes were pushed together like a bedraggled, retreating army. He'd left almost everything behind when he moved out. He owned a lot of woollen jumpers – argyle ones, with wool so heavy it looked like it'd been knitted by a giant's needles. He also had a lot of flannel shirts.

"Oy," yelled your Grand Mar the first time she saw me in one of them. "What the hell are you wearing? Take that off now! You look homeless!"

The tutoring was in the community centre, a squat building with brown industrial carpet, four meeting rooms and a big wooden-floored space you could hire for sports and cheap sixtieth birthdays and twenty-firsts. A paper sign stuck onto the brick wall of the foyer pointed the way to *Free Homework Help – Room 3. Begins today.*

Except for the beam of light from the front window where the dust motes swam like airborne plankton, the corridor was prison-dark. I heard noise coming from one room and headed there. A peeling brown trestle table stood in the corner. On top were three cardboard boxes filled with books – raggedy ones with distressed cloth covers, like beggars looking for a good home. *FREE bOOks*, someone had written in texta on one box.

Five nails bloomed on the wall, like distant and embarrassed relatives, planted there long before the invention of Blu Tack. There was a yellowy *Life. Be in it* poster with lazy Norm looking quizzically at the viewer with a bottle of beer in his hand. Benign, like my dad. Not those go-getter, "Life – what's in it *for me*?" sorts. I wasn't trying to be grandular or anything. I was under no illusion that this crappy room the colour and reek of smoker's teeth was going to change my life.

I found a chair by an empty table and sat down. Seven other people were in the class. One was Vinny, who lived in a flat four floors below ours. I would see him sometimes taking his little sister to the playground. There were also two Filipino girls, who'd named themselves Violet and Cherry after their favourite chocolate bars, and a few others I didn't know but whose faces seemed familiar. Vinny, Cherry and Violet were starting Year Nine, while the youngest kid looked like she was in Grade Six.

Someone tall was leaning over Violet. "No, I don't think your teacher wanted you to write an essay about young people in Tokyo," he was telling her.

"But she said write about youth in Asia for holiday homework," Violet insisted.

"Euthanasia, Violet."

"Yes," Violet agreed, "so I'm writing about Children's Day in Japan."

I stood up to leave. There was no way I was hanging out in Homework Help like some stupid kept-back-a-year kid. I couldn't see a single student here my age.

"Oh, we have a newcomer." He'd finally noticed me. His face set me on edge; it was one of those faces where a few millimetres made the difference between handsome and odd, the sort of face that might shift between each state depending on the day, or the mood.

I took off your Grand Par's cap, and he looked surprised to find I was a girl. "I'm Karuna."

He seemed baffled. "I'm sorry." There was a pause. "Are you here to help me . . . ?"

"No. I'm a student."

I could see the relief on his face – he didn't want another tutor meddling with his class.

"What year are you in, Carina?"

"Year Eleven. It's Karuna."

"Karuna. Hmm, that's an interesting name. What is it? Spanish? Indian?" He was doing what a lot of people did, thinking they were being so cleverly tactful instead of full-on transparent, trying to work out my face from my name.

"Pali," I replied.

"Pali?"

"Yes, the language of early Buddhism."

"I know what Pali is," he replied. "I was just surprised . . ."

"That I would know the origin of my own name?"

He was embarrassed now, but it served him right, to come in assuming we were all stupid just because we lived in crappy concrete places, and that he knew our names better than we did ourselves.

"So, *Karuna*, what does your name mean in Pali?"

It was humiliating, the name my mother had given me, her insistence that my father accept it, even if he wanted to raise me Catholic.

"Compassion," I replied.

"Cool," he said. Then he saw the look on my face. "No, really, it's cool." He grinned. "Hey, at least you weren't named Sweet Charity."

I decided he was okay, not one of those earnest do-gooders.

"Are you looking for High School Survival Tools? Because that program doesn't start until late February."

"What's that?"

"My older brother is gonna go," Vinny chimed in. "It's for your last two years. Will you be the tutor there too?"

"Nah, mate, I'll be in Adelaide by then."

"Awww."

Of course a class named Homework Help was not for Year Eleven students. He must have thought I was intellectually slow, but now I thought of the huge blank that was my summer break.

I sat back down and took out my Biology textbook. I didn't need to ask for his name, because every five minutes some kid would call it out. "Ray! Ray, I need help with this."

Ray, a drop of golden sun. Even though he was the one circling around the room.

But of course, I never asked him for any help.

It was almost comforting, being in there with those kids. I put away my biology book and pulled out *The Handmaid's Tale*, a newish book we were going to be studying. A couple of times Ray walked past me, but didn't say anything.

Did I like him? I wasn't sure. Wasn't this the question we were supposed to ask ourselves whenever we encountered a cute boy in our orbit? All I knew was that I liked being in that room with him while he tried to ignore me. I had a feeling it wouldn't last long. Sure enough, during his next rotation he leaned over to ask me what I was reading. I showed him the cover.

"Some kind of fairytale?" he asked.

"Not really."

I liked it when he loitered nearby. I liked the attention. Even though I knew I had not earned it in any way, this was the only superpower I had and I'd gotten it simply by going through puberty.

"Do you need a lift?" he asked hesitantly, after everyone had left and I was still there, reading about Offred's secret meetings with her lover, which were disappointingly the opposite of sexy.

I nodded.

"Okay, sure, I'll drive you home. Where do you live?"

"The flats."

I knew what he was thinking – I could have walked the seven minutes home. But before he could decide I was Mustang Sally with my fat feet looking for a free ride in a fast car, I said, "You asked if I needed a lift somewhere."

"But not home?"

"No."

I thought he might try to act all social worker on me: *What is wrong at home? Does your school know? Do you have support?*

But he didn't. In his eye was a glint.

"Okay," he said, walking me to his silver magnet of a car. "Where would you like me to take you? A relative's house? The library? The supermarket?" He started up the engine and I thought of how much your Grand Par would appreciate the lungs on this vehicle.

"Nowhere particular. Just go." I didn't ask if he had more important stuff to do. I didn't worry whether he wanted to or not. I wouldn't have cared if he'd told me to get out of the car. No one in life gives you a free ride, your Grand Par had told me once, but here I was and I would milk it for all it was worth. Boys like this didn't drop by every day.

His air freshener was shaped like a flower, and he had a Care Bear in the rear window. On the back seat there was a massive, rigid, purple bunny with long-lashed eyes – the sort of toy you'd win at a carnival.

"Do you have a little sister?" I asked.

"Nah, I'm an only child." He paused. "The police kept pulling me over, thinking I'd stolen this car. I was sick of always explaining, having to pull out my ID and crap like that. So I got these toys to make it look more like a family car. It must have worked because the cops have only pulled me over once since. They must get me mixed up with the drug dealers all over the news."

"Eh?"

"Brown skin, squinty eyes. We all look the same."

"You don't have squinty eyes."

"Ha, thanks, Molly Ringwald. Hey, how about now?" He narrowed his eyes. "Do I look like Long Duk Dong?"

"Who?"

"'What's happenin', hot stuff?'"

"I have no idea what you're talking about."

"You don't go to the movies much, do you?"

"No."

When we were on the road, he asked, "Do you really need homework help?"

"Dunno. I haven't started Year Eleven yet. My mum's boss told my mum and she made me come."

"What do you want to do when you finish school?"

"Dunno," I replied. I knew I sounded stupid, but I didn't want to make up a lie to impress him.

Then he started talking about himself. He'd always wanted to be a doctor, he said. The idea of being able to fix bodies that were breaking down seemed like some kind of small miracle of God. He actually said that: *miracle of God*. I wondered whether he was some kind of religious nut. His parents reckoned he would be the next José Rizal.

"Who's that?" I asked. I'd never been this close to a boy before, without either my mother or a friend sitting between us. I felt bizarrely calm.

Apparently, José Rizal was some kind of Filipino national hero – a doctor, artist and writer. They shot him for one of his novels, some book with a Latin name that meant "Touch Me Not".

"My mum's from the Philippines," I told him.

"Really? And she never told you about Rizal?"

"She's Chinese and she can't read," I said.

"But there are statues of him all over Manila."

"Yeah, my mum was pretty ghetto, I think," I said. "She just hung around with Chinese kids in her local neighbourhood. In fact, my great-grandfather was the first in our family to arrive in the Philippines, and for three generations our bloodline was pure Chinese. Until my dad came along and messed things up."

We must have cruised the wilds of Albion, Deer Park, St Albans and Sunshine for an hour before he asked, "Home now?"

"Just drop me back at the community centre. I can walk from there."

"You are one mysterious young lady."

"Not really. I just don't want my mum to know I've been riding around with strange boys in foreign cars."

His laugh, head flung back, was like a jagged cartoon-bubble laugh. *Har ha ha ha har.* The next scene was the back of his Mercedes driving away, yellow Funshine Bear smiling his raised-eyebrow smile at me from the back window.

Ray, a drop of golden sun.
Me, a name I call myself.
Far, a long, long way to run.

It continued like this for two more weeks: me turning up to the community centre with a novel and sitting there, reading, and then us going for a ride around the streets of my hood for about an hour. He probably wondered why I couldn't have just read at home. But there was something comforting about being around those kids, full of earnest ambition. And of course, I liked being near Ray, so unlike the boys around here who slouched and mumbled monosyllables – even the nicer, more driven ones like Vincent and his brother. Here, parents and children didn't have conversations – your parents told you what to do and you did it. There was nothing to discuss, so no one had taught us how to talk.

The other thing about Ray was his smell – so clean, so fresh, like how I imagined a man in a toothpaste ad would smell. The sort of smell of someone who came from wide-walled, white-tiled houses with marble benchtops and walk-in wardrobes.

"You're a smart girl. You really should make plans for the future," he said to me one afternoon before he started the car.

I shrugged. I wished he'd just keep talking about himself, like he had for the past two weeks – not because I was one of those girls who gaped in awe at everything a boy said, but because it took the attention away from me.

"You have a lot of potential." He told me he could tell I was intelligent and curious about the big, wide world. But all he'd ever seen me do was sit there, reading. I did that mainly to block out the wider world, which at times felt like a bleak run into emptiness.

"You like books. You should go to university. You could study literature."

"Ha!" I could not have thought of anything more pointless. "I only want to *read* books. Not study them."

"Maybe you could *write* them," he suggested, in the same way a Grade Four teacher might suggest you become an astronaut because you drew a lovely picture of space. What would I write about? I'd never read a book about someone like me. Characters like me didn't exist because my life wasn't interesting, not even to myself. I knew the routine. He was just pretending I was fascinating because he found me attractive.

"How old are you?" he suddenly asked.

"Sixteen. What about you?"

"Turning nineteen in May."

He seemed so much older, because he knew where he was going.

"You know, you seem pretty mature for a sixt—"

To shut him up, I leaned over and kissed him.

To my surprise, even though I had never been in an aeroplane before, my stomach felt like it was in flight.

Tweezer would call this kind of feeling a crush, but I thought

a crush sounded like an awful predicament: squashed, broken
into little pieces; a word you'd find on a drink carton to describe
sour fruits. This definitely was not a crush, having less to do with
the yielding feelings of romance and more to do with pouncing
animal longing. Romance was a waste of time. I was not going
to fall in love and expect Prince Charming to save me. I knew
Ray found me delightful, but so had your Grand Par, and that
hadn't stopped him from leaving. Girls like me didn't stop men
from carrying on with their lives.

I may have been in the passenger seat, but I knew exactly
what I was doing.

It didn't happen straight after the first kiss, of course – me and
your father in the back of the Merc, like the most clichéd teenage
movie about a rich boy and a poor girl, the prince and pauperess.
Obviously he never set foot inside our flat. Imagine him seeing
the double bed strewn with your Grand Mar's pyjamas, the Tiger
Balm oil on the bedside table, my leggings on a chair.

There were far worse places to pop a cherry. Kylie popped
hers in a cinema while *Weird Science* was showing, Wendy in
the primary school playground at night, Shalini in the back
storeroom of Luis's dad's grocery store while his dad visited
a lady who was not Luis's mother. They were all drunk on the
shaken-up fizzy drink of love. *Pop! Pop! Pop!* Suddenly it was
happening all over the place, all at once. Red starbursts in spots
we had never intended for those explosions to happen. After all,
velvet pillows and satin-sheet fantasies were for those with more
money and privacy and less interfering parents.

So there we were, two weeks after that first kiss, still with most of our clothes on as far as any passing voyeur could see, except we had smished ourselves into one hot, rocking, caramel mass.

He was like a puppy afterwards, wanting to nuzzle, to pet and be petted. He turned the motor on, fidgeted with the air conditioning, a silly, shy grin on his face. If I hadn't been in his car, I would have wanted to raise a triumphant fist in the air. Woohoo! I'd conquered something. I had no posse of friends to confide in, but it also meant that my experience remained true and unsullied by the giddy expectations of others or the dagger eyes of your Grand Mar. It was mine and mine alone. It didn't make me a "woman", but it made me feel like a separate person with secrets. It made me feel, piece by piece, myself – thought and deed.

"So – are you on the pill or something?"

I was surprised he had let it go all the way. I hadn't bled, and he didn't ask me why. Even I didn't know. But he seemed to think I knew what I was doing – which, come to think of it, said a lot about what he thought of me. Pretty ghetto, like my mum.

Your Grand Mar would never let me be on the pill, even though Dr Lee had recommended it for my terrible period pain. "It messes up your insides," she had told me. "You'll never be able to have children in the future if you take it."

A seed of worry started to sprout, but I buried it in the back of my mind.

"Yes," I lied, looking him in the eye.

He began to button up my shirt. "So," he smirked, "is this your ex-boyfriend's?"

"No. My dad's."

He gave me a strange look, but said nothing.

*

When I got home, I went immediately to the bathroom. Crouching on the floor of the shower, I unscrewed our bottle of Dettol and douched myself using the small plastic syringe your Grand Mar had kept from a long-ago-used-up bottle of medicine. In Dr Lee's waiting room I'd once read a story in an ancient *Women's Weekly* magazine about a woman who successfully used a disinfectant called Lysol as a contraceptive during the Great Depression. I figured that Dettol was the same thing, and I knew it was working for me by the way it stung.

Afterwards, still worried your Grand Mar could smell the pheromones floating around me like blaring music that only I could hear, I took a long hot shower.

Your Grand Mar found me sitting on the floor in front of our coffee table with my History textbook open. I could tell she was pleased. I was a good girl, soft and quiet. The only noise I made was the turning of a page, the only force I used was to press a ballpoint pen onto the lined page of an exercise book.

That evening in bed, I lay curled on my side, legs bent and swung away from your Grand Mar. My body no longer felt like it belonged to her, a project to be carved out and polished up. It did not belong to Ray, either. I was my own instrument. I pulled my own strings.

For once, joy was a fog that laid low – low enough for me to float around in, as I squeezed grey water out of our mop, as

I carried a laundry basket and a cupful of detergent to the communal washing machines near the stairwell. Joy swirled around my knees and filled the corners of our flat, so that instead of noticing dark lines of mould around our kitchen tiles, I saw the gold that filtered in our window before dusk, felt the warmth on my bare arms.

I knew I was so bad, but I felt treacherously, lecherously good, to the point where I also felt so sorry for your old Grand Mar, knowing she'd probably never in her entire life felt so good. She believed this goodness only happened to people without freckles. How wrong she was. An older man was falling for me, and I had done it all myself, in defiance of everything your Grand Mar had ever taught me.

"You feel terrific," Ray said as he stroked my skin.

I know, I thought, it's true. I do feel terrific.

I didn't have anything to lose like Ray did. No one imagined a bright future for me, a future where I could be a doctor-novelist national hero worthy of assassination. I wasn't going to pine for him when he was gone. I wouldn't let myself fall in love. I would not cling, like your Grand Mar, red-faced and red-eyed, had clung to your Grand Par by his sleeve and cuff, hollering, "Don't you dare leave me!" Because people did leave; people were filled with indifferent daring, daring that had nothing to do with how you felt or how white-knuckled your grip was.

Your Grand Par had said to me once, "I don't like how your mother dangles you like jailbait in front of all those boys." This was after your Grand Mar had wistfully remarked that my distant cousin Marcus in Los Angeles had just got into dentistry.

"Sick," said your Grand Par, "youse Asians are sick. You can't set her up with family. Besides, she's only fourteen!"

Your Grand Mar just glared at him, saying nothing.

I had sided with your Grand Par, because he came to my defence in these things – he confirmed my suspicions that your Grand Mar's hidden plans for me were dodgy and unnatural. Like a porcelain ornament in a cheap gift shop, I was to be kept behind glass – *look but don't touch!* Your Grand Mar may have been blind to how little I was really worth, but I wasn't. I knew the truth. She had grossly inflated my value, hoping a gullible buyer would come along and be so dazzled that before he had time to reassess, I would be wed and ballooning with new life. I knew that if she met Ray, she would probably be very pleased. Her ruse would have worked.

On the last day of Homework Help, when all the other kids had gone, Ray stood at the trestle table, in front of the free books. "Hey, here's one for you," he said, handing me a book so old that its cover was the same colour as the faded photograph of a storm on the wall, some long-ago art project. "You'll like it, mestizo muse."

"What is this?" I opened it up. Poems. I closed it. *Walt Whitman* was written on the spine. "I don't read poetry," I told him.

"You think it's a wanky thing to do, don't you?" he asked.

"I don't get most of it. Don't know what's good or bad."

"Just think of each line of a poem like a shelf," he told me, "and each word is like a thing on that shelf. A good poet chooses their objects carefully. What you want to end up with is not a single thing on that shelf that should not be there. I think that's what makes a poem good." He pointed to the book. "I'd be interested to know what you make of it."

I took Walt Whitman. I hadn't got him anything.

"Do you need a lift back?" he asked, now our shorthand for going elsewhere.

"Yes, please."

He got in the car, I got in the passenger seat, and he drove. His car smelt like the new pair of leather shoes your Grand Par had bought for his mother's funeral.

Ray parked in the empty cricket pitch car park two blocks away from the community centre.

Our last time.

He looked at me, and I knew what that look meant. It was the same look your Grand Par gave me before he left. He didn't want to break my heart, for me to moon after him like an abandoned pup hungry for hugs. He was scared that I was attached, me being so young. Ray didn't know I wasn't thinking of abandonment, because I didn't belong to him, and I didn't expect him to take me anywhere beyond those short car trips.

"Don't worry," I said, "you've already given me this cheap-arse book. I don't want anything else from you." It was supposed to be a joke, but when it came out of my mouth it sounded bitter.

He dropped me back at the community centre so I could walk the seven minutes back to our flats.

Our home also smelled and felt like the inside of a shoe, but a synthetic pair of runners at the back of a mothball-cupboard. I sat down on our brown couch, opened the Walt Whitman and looked at the first line.

I celebrate myself.

*

I knew by the end of the summer he would be gone and everything that had happened to me would be like a dream, but it was still hard when the next week rolled by and the thing I had been looking forward to most was no longer there. I did not think of our time together in the way of those surreal sepia montages they always show in movies, but in small concrete things: the down on his ear, the smell of his air freshener, the blur of the suburbs from his car window.

I kept reading the Whitman. This guy wrote in the same way my mind seemed to meander these days, his sentences ending before his thoughts did, his ideas jumping from cliffs to valleys and then skinny-dipping in rivers before emerging, finger-and-toeing up mountains. The man was mad, couldn't think in a straight line, but he knew about multitudes, all the different sorts a self could be. All these spongy cells that are compelled to unite even as they will be destroyed by the worm of time.

Every evening I'd tuck the book in the space between the wall and the cupboard. I suppose it didn't really matter if your Grand Mar saw the Whitman, because she'd just assume it was a schoolbook. But when you have been raised to cough up everything you have, you get pretty good at hiding things you don't want taken away.

Chapter 5

didn't think Corindirk State School would be that different, but boy, was I wrong. The Greek girls here wore blue eyeshadow, puffed their hair up and had a lot of gold on their fingers, wrists and necks. Instead of retreating, they advanced like a battalion. I suspected they were the sort of girl Tweezer had wanted to be all along, if she hadn't been so pathologically shy, and if all modern fashion and cosmetics had not been denied her.

"Hello," I called out to a cluster of them I met on the first day. No teacher here had assigned anyone to help me settle in, so I had to make an effort. They didn't answer me.

"Hey," I tried again.

I'd wanted to find another Tweezer, not realising that girls like Tweezer would only come to me, not the other way around.

"I'm sorry, were you talking to me?" The shortest of the five girls glared at me. I'd slighted them without realising why or how.

"Yeah, the lezzo's talking to you, Petra," said her friend.

I finally got it. Because there was no uniform here, every thread on every body was noted and analysed. And I'd thought kids at co-ed state schools cared least about these things. My jeans and oversized T-shirt did not pass muster with these ultra-feminine girls.

"Geez, I'd hate to be up myself," one of them muttered as I walked past the next day, and that was that. I decided that I wasn't going to like this shitty place, with its rules I had no clue about, and that I would do my best to escape it, if not in body then in mind. With Tweezer I had a simple friendship – when I was with her I felt the same as I did when alone, but better. But at this place, none of them could imagine a family like mine. Sure, plenty of the skip girls had divorced parents, but their mums became their best friends, with tantrums and silent treatments on both sides. They weren't living in your Grand Mar's medieval world, with its stone walls.

"Come home straight after school," your Grand Mar warned me. "You have the key to the flat. You know how to get dinner ready. Don't dither, and don't hang around the playground." The playground at the bottom of our flats was just a skeletal monkey-bar set and a tunnel slide graffitied over with inflated, permanent-marker genitals. I had no idea why your Grand Mar thought this would appeal to me, at sixteen.

The other thing that put me off the new school was that I had to see the guidance officer once a fortnight, a woman with too much white eyeliner on her inner eye-rims and a habit of touching my shoulder or hand while staring at me intently and saying, "How do you *feel* about that?" I would look out her window at the leaves on the eucalyptus tree, and imagine Jareth the Goblin King perched up there, beckoning me away to the labyrinth. The guidance officer probably had no idea what to make of my secret smile. I never harboured such fantasies about Ray because I knew he would never beckon me away.

Now there was no Tweezer to fill the quiet with her dreams of the future. I had never met a girl who had such optimism despite all evidence to the contrary – her home life, her strict parents, her circumscribed days. I had to breathe oxygen into my own dreams.

I knew that my thoughts went wandering because I hated being stuck. It didn't have anything to do with your Grand Par leaving. I was just glad he wasn't here to see these changes in me.

My period was three days late.

Suppose the Dettol hadn't worked, I thought. Suppose I was carrying Ray's baby. Ha! I would really have something over your Grand Mar – a small, good thing, smaller than an apple seed. It would be another secret. Secret by secret I would build myself up, I thought, until I would be completely unknowable to your Grand Mar, until she could no longer remember the Me that was before.

There would be two of us, against her. I would be a good mum. I would not stare at your face looking for something to fix. Maybe we could move in with your Grand Par. I wouldn't even tell Ray that he had a baby, because I wouldn't want to stress him out in the first year of medical school. I would raise you and then, when you were four or five, he'd fly back, a fully-fledged doctor. He'd meet you and be so grateful for my stoic silence that he would marry me and you'd be the flower girl. Then this housing commission Cinderella would be out of here, swept away in his car with the warm seats, to a life in a safe suburb where the autumn leaves on the ground would be bigger than my palm and as crisp as twenty-dollar notes, not crumbly and sooty and possibly covered in dog shit like the leaves in the park at the bottom of the flats.

Every part of me felt so hot all the time, like I was a soft loaf out of an oven. My right eyeball seemed to breathe condensation on my sunglasses. My hands and feet felt like little fire-pads. I wished that Ray were here, so we could make the most of it, skin on skin. Of course, I couldn't be pregnant, otherwise I wouldn't be feeling this randy. If I were pregnant, sex would probably be the last thing on my mind instead of the first thing every morning. I wouldn't be she-bopping with my hands down my pants after your Grand Mar had left the bed to prepare breakfast. I'd be feeling vomity and craving pickles.

Yet every day, for three days, I added new details to this fantasy, in the way that Tweezer had shown me. I gave myself a brick house with wall-to-wall carpet, and a job writing short stories for *Reader's Digest*.

When I first came across your Grand Par's *Reader's Digest*s, I had thought that the title referred to how the reader's brain had to break the stories into small pieces and absorb them like food. Your Grand Par just laughed and said, "Tool Kitty, you are a poet as well as a handyman." Only later did I realise that it was called *Reader's Digest* because most of the articles in the magazine were shortened versions of existing stories. I could do that, I thought. I'd have time to do the thing I loved most – read – and make my favourite stories easier to read for people who probably didn't have time. That, to me, would be a *real* job, and real writing, not pointless essays about the meaning of Margaret Atwood's dystopias.

Then I woke up on Monday morning and found some bloody spots in my underwear.

I knew it. The fantasy was too much. I had imagined the life out of it, and now it was spluttering out its last protests. Keep it in your pants, those bright wet spots were saying to me. Keep it in. Your bloody pants. No genius baby for me, no getting out of this suburb, no happy exciting thing just on the cusp of happening. Drab flat, mediocre marks at school, and now even my own body was hostile, not giving me a single month more to milk every drop from my stupid fantasy.

There were no cramps, but I filled up a hot water bottle and held it beneath my belly button anyway. When I was thirteen, I'd created a chart called *My Periodic Table*, which had nothing to do with the elements and everything to do with how often I bled. My own body was like a machine I didn't have a user manual for.

That evening I dozed off on the couch, dreaming of dates and calendars filled with red ink, dripping onto our bed, steeping our sheets, until your Grand Mar was swimming in a sea, head barely above water, telling me, "Look what I bought!", laughing, and holding up a plastic bag . . .

She was swinging a bag of Kentucky Fried Chicken above my head when I opened my eyes. "Put on the rice cooker," she said. Fried chicken was a special treat, and we always had to have it with rice, because your Grand Mar wanted me to fill up on more rice than chicken. "Chicken makes you fat," she said. "Just like those Australians who eat it from the bucket, in front of the television."

She wondered aloud why I looked so dour, why I wasn't

moving, until she saw the hot water bottle on my belly. "It's okay," she said. "I'll put on the rice. Just rest."

The happy fog had now turned into a heavy fatigue. Walking back from school was like wading through a soporific sludge, and all I wanted to do when I got home every afternoon was climb into bed and sleep, so that my waking life and dreaming life became a blur. I'd never felt so exhausted. Maybe it was the loss of the phantom baby, maybe it was the prospect of a whole year without Ray to look forward to. Used up – that's how I felt.

I developed an obsession that brought me some small comfort. I would pull the lid off a texta and hold it close to my nose. Delicious. Like the smell of nail polish, but better. My favourite smell of all was new whiteboard markers, so soft and mallowy in a chemical way. I'd stolen one from an unsuspecting teacher who'd forgotten to pack it up after class, and spent hours lying on my side in bed, sniffing and reading, swallowing or being swallowed by – I didn't know which – a thick slurry of fatigue.

The days stretched as they had before, flaccid like balloons blown up too many times without their knots tied. They'd lost their buoyancy, become no fun. *Love's Labour's Lost*, I sometimes thought deliriously. It was the name of the play we would study this year after the grim *Handmaid*. Nothing was ever going to happen to me again. Whatever I'd done with Ray seemed to have sucked the life out of me.

"When was the last time your monthlies came?" your Grand Mar suddenly asked me one night, when I thought she was already asleep.

Of all the kids in my Grade Six class, I was the only one whose mum ticked the *NO* box on the permission slips for the school nurse to come and explain human reproduction. While the rest of the class got to find out, I was put in with the Grade Fours, listening to Mrs Morgan re-read *The BFG*. At Christ Our Saviour, we'd studied the reproductive system in Year Nine Science, but that was all about fallopian tubes and ovaries and sperm – what I really needed to know was, if you've had your period, can you still grow a baby? But of course I couldn't be pregnant – otherwise your Grand Mar would have rooted it out already, like a truffle pig in a documentary I saw on telly.

She was asking too late, when there was nothing for her to get worked up about, just disappointment and depression on my end. Two and a half months since our deeds, and two short visits from the Red Lady. Both times, she arrived on very lightly treading legs, leaving only a faint blood-print.

Chapter 6

And then I knew.

The third month nothing came at all, and I was bloated, but in a way I had never been before – instead of pudding-like, the skin of my stomach felt tight and stretched like a drum. One morning, when I opened the fridge to get the orange juice, I felt an urge to throw up.

And then I became a useless superhero with the superpower of smell. The world was attacking me through scents. They threw themselves at me thick and fast. Inside the supermarket, all the packages of food were leaning forward, exhaling their warm, fetid MSG breath. Outside, cooking oil from the corner take-away joint clogged up my nostrils and made me want to hurl into the drain. Even the rain would launch unexpected assaults, a sudden attack of soggy wattle or drenched garbage.

I had the feeling this nausea was meant to happen early on, immediately, and not three months in. Something was not right with my body.

I have to tell Ray, I thought.

But I'd already had my period twice. What if half of the baby had leaked out of me already and what was left inside was a semi-deformed dumpling of a thing? Only a real doctor could answer my questions, but there was no way I would go and ask Dr Lee, a man older than my father who still liked to tickle me under the armpits after every injection. I couldn't go to him with my sordid problems. He'd tell your Grand Mar.

I started to shower immediately after I returned from school, instead of in the evenings, because there was no way I could let her find out. Your Grand Mar felt free to barge into the bathroom any time she needed to retrieve her toothbrush, or a towel, or just to remind me to do something. Because she had made me, she felt my body belonged to her, that there was nothing she hadn't seen or that could be hidden from her.

You didn't seem real back then, because I thought I'd feel a little feral animal moving around. Since I could sometimes feel and hear food digesting in my stomach, I thought you'd feel like a large bit of meat, with lumpy limbs prodding at my insides. My tummy didn't feel very much except bloated.

Maybe, I thought, you might exist, but you might also cease to exist. Maybe I might have a heavy bleed, by accident, and then you'd be gone. Better not make a drama out of nothing yet. Crazy, I know, but that's what I was thinking.

I remembered how in Science class last year, Mr Vo had told us that all human life was made of carbon, oxygen, hydrogen, calcium and a few other elements I'd already forgotten. He said that scientists could figure out the percentages of each kind of matter in our body and the exact composition of cells, but they could never figure out how to animate those cells to make them come to life; and yet every second our bodies were already doing it.

Just like breathing. We barely think about it but when we

do, breathing becomes extremely difficult. Like it did at the thought of your Grand Mar finding out about you. This made each breath speed up and crash into the next one. What would she do to me when she found out? Forget my thoughts, even my body wouldn't belong to me. Maybe she would make me get rid of you. Tweezer had told me that doctors could scrape out babies with spoons, not that I wanted to be taking medical wisdom from someone whose love interests – Sleeping Beauty's Prince Phillip, Ricky Martin – would never get her in this state.

One evening, I must have kicked the blankets off myself in a hot frenzy, and a corner of drummy skin must have peeped through my pyjama top, because suddenly I felt your Grand Mar's hands on my shoulders, shaking me awake, slowly at first, but then roughly, like she was trying to shake a fire off me.

"Whaa . . . ?" I asked groggily, sitting up.

"Lift up your top," she commanded.

"No."

"Do it. Now!"

There was no getting out of this. I did as I was told.

She looked at my belly for a long time. "How did this happen?" she asked, quietly.

I didn't say anything. I couldn't look at her face.

"When did this happen? How long has it been?"

I told her I didn't know.

"Are you stupid or what?" screamed your Grand Mar. "How can you not know? What is wrong with you?" She took me by the shoulders as if she could rattle the truth out of me. "Who did this?"

I lay curled away from your Grand Mar, eyes wide open, fingernail in mouth. I knew we both wouldn't be getting any sleep that night.

Your Grand Mar called Mrs Osman first thing the next morning. "I too sick to come in," she rasped, and she really did sound like she had coughed out half a lung, because she had spent most of the night screaming at me like a hyena in a trap.

Then we took a bus straight to the Maribyrnong Medical Centre.

"She have a baby!" your Grand Mar yelled at the triage nurse in Emergency.

The nurse's eyes shot straight to my belly. "Are you miscarrying?"

"I don't know what that means."

"Are you losing your baby?"

"I don't know." I wasn't sure whether this was going to be my decision.

"Are you bleeding right now?"

"No."

"Do you have any pains?"

"No."

"Are you vomiting too much?"

"No."

"Do you have a high fever?"

"No."

"What's wrong then, love?"

"I'm just pregnant," I said. *Just pregnant.*

"I see." She didn't see at all. "Were you assaulted?"

"No!"

Your Grand Mar glared at me.

"Sorry," I said to the nurse. "My mum made me come here. She wanted me to see a doctor." We both had black bags under our eyes big enough to carry the suburb's garbage, with room to spare.

"Oh," said the nurse finally. "It's your first time seeing a doctor for pregnancy." She sighed. "I'm afraid that's the role of your GP. Do you have a family doctor you can see? They will make a referral to the local hospital. Generally that's how it works. Your GP can discuss your pregnancy options with you."

Your Grand Mar declared to the nurse: "Nurse, she was trick! A boy trick her! She won't tell me who it is because she scared."

I turned to your Grand Mar. "The nurse says we have to see our own doctor," I told her, even though I knew she understood.

Your Grand Mar was muttering behind my back like a crazy bat, repeating what she had said during the night, but in a low monotone. "Like hell we'll go and see Dr Lee, who's known you since you were born. Might as well just kill me now, peel the skin from my head like a pomegranate, I'll lose so much face because of my whore of a daughter. Til Ner Seng!" And she thought that *I* was the embarrassment to society.

Another nurse, who had been working in the background, stood up. She had permed hair the colour of a black texta, and when she spoke, she showed as much gum as teeth.

"Sister, ay, sister." She beckoned your Grand Mar over with a curled finger.

Your Grand Mar's head shot up – it was rare to meet another person speaking our language.

"Stop cursing our gods. What's done is done." Perm Nurse turned to the first nurse and explained, "Donna, I'm just translating for the mum here."

"Oh, okay, Chin. You deal with this one, then."

"Come," commanded Nurse Chin, "step aside from the window so you don't hold up the other people waiting in line."

Emerging from the triage station, Nurse Chin walked towards us. She and your Grand Mar were exactly the same height. "There's a doctor two streets from this hospital. I'll write down her address and phone number. See her today and she will get a referral for your daughter to the public hospital system."

"Thank you, thank you, nurse," said your Grand Mar. "Aiyooh, you understand. My daughter was tricked by a boy! Wah, woe, the horror!"

"Do you know how many stupid teenagers are out there?" Nurse Chin said now, her voice suddenly quiet, like a slowly spreading, barely detectable deadly gas. "You can't just march into a public hospital demanding valuable emergency services just because you don't want to lose face in front of your own doctor. Do you think your doctor hasn't seen this sort of crap before? Do you think he goes home and thinks about your family all night long? He does not. He eats dinner, watches TV and sleeps before he wakes up the next morning to see a new lot of patients. The only time he would stress about your daughter is if you brought her in half-dying because you were stupid enough to hide her pregnancy for so long. Now go away and see this GP, and don't ever humiliate us like that again!"

They spoke the same language alright, Nurse Chin and your Grand Mar. They were probably around the same age too. But

Nurse Chin was a professional behind a white desk in a hospital, who'd probably worked hard to get to where she was, and to make people forget *what* she was. She reminded me of the brainy, proud Asian girls at school, the ones who knew they'd be dentists and lawyers and didn't bother befriending anyone who wasn't going to be of that calibre. Just when Nurse Chin least expected it, along came this demanding peasant yakking away about her daughter being duped, like this was a chickenshit village instead of a big world where smart Asian women could get opportunity and independence. She had contempt for your Grand Mar, but couldn't help splashing it onto me too.

"What a crazy bitch," muttered your Grand Mar as soon as we were out the door. "It'll serve you right if she's the one to deliver the baby when it comes. *Don't humiliate us again!* She was the one doing the humiliating. I have never been so humiliated in my life. Fuck her gods."

I thought about what your Grand Mar had just said – *deliver the baby*. I assumed she'd marched me to the hospital to see what could be done about getting rid of it. In fact, I'd resigned myself to the idea. Her hollering for five hours straight last night was enough to make anyone want to put a hole through their own skull or stomach. I was surprised the neighbours hadn't called the cops with the amount of noise your Grand Mar had made.

"Who the hell will take care of it?" she had croaked, pacing our bedroom, just as daylight crept in. "You're still a child, you can't even take care of yourself. I will have to look after it. Instead of making life easier for your Mah, you keep making problems for me!"

"Fine, I'll get rid of it then. I hope that'll make you happy."

She yanked me by the shoulders. "Are you crazy? You think it's so easy that they just use a vacuum cleaner to suck it out?"

"Then what do you want me to do?"

She hadn't answered, just resumed her screeching, as I gazed at our stippled ceiling and blocked her out. If I had the choice, I thought, I'd keep the baby. At least I'd have something of my own.

From the medical centre we walked the two blocks to a little grey office with DR G. MASANO in big silver letters stuck on the window. There were four patients before us, and a stack of dog-eared magazines on a laminex table. I picked one up. *Be BOLD!* declared the cover of *Dolly*, *Be the bravest you!* Turns out that to be the bravest you, all you had to do was wear orange with purple. I flipped the page and looked at an ad. *Never underestimate the power of a scented candle!* I had never realised how ridiculous these magazines were. I remembered Tweezer poring over them in the school library, like they were scientific journals containing the cure to her unpopularity – perhaps the right eyeliner application would change her life.

Not mine. It turned out that I was almost four months along.

"Spotting happens," Dr Masano said, when we were finally called into her office and I told her that I'd had blood in my underpants only a few months ago. Her desk was crowded with yellow folders, and a plastic model of a uterus balanced precariously on top of one stack. "We still don't know why. But they were definitely not periods. You can't get your period when you are pregnant." She reminded me of one of those teachers you were shit-scared of, but respected.

"Who did this?" your Grand Mar demanded of the doctor, as if she knew.

"If Karuna is not ready to tell you, Mrs Kelly, then I'm afraid you'll just have to wait until she is."

This was an outrage to your Grand Mar – when a parent demanded something of you, you had to do it straightaway.

"You know what?" Dr Masano looked directly at your Grand Mar. "Let me talk to Karuna alone, if you don't mind."

I knew your Grand Mar only agreed because she thought Dr Masano could extract a name from me.

After your Grand Mar left, Dr Masano turned to me with her serious brown eyes. "Do you know the father of your child? Would you like to file a police report?"

"No! I know who it is." I looked down at my hands, embarrassed, even though I knew that Dr Masano probably encountered a hundred teenagers like me every year. "He's just not around anymore."

"How old was he?"

"Eighteen."

She looked at me kindly. "What support will you have to look after this baby?"

"My mother," I replied automatically. I knew what the doctor was implying. "I don't want to give it away." The truth was, if I'd had a reason – a more exciting life, if I had been a whizz at school and had a brilliant future ahead of me – I might have given the baby up.

"I'm going to send you to pathology to get some blood tests," she said, "and send off some forms to make sure you'll be in the public hospital system." She outlined the appointments I would have from now until the baby was born. "Okay," she said to me, "let's see if we can listen to your baby's heartbeat."

And that's when I heard your galloping heart for the first time, lying on that narrow bed in Dr Masano's office.

"If you tell me, we can work out a way to make him pay," said your Grand Mar when we got home. Make him pay in a way she'd failed to do with your Grand Par.

But I would never tell her. I didn't want to be married off at sixteen and spend the rest of my days waiting hand and foot on a boy I barely knew.

I felt so stupid. How could I not have known? How did your Grand Mar not detect it earlier? "I only had one baby – you," she told me. "I wasn't popping them out one after another every year, like my mother did." I had been absolutely sure that your Grand Mar would have known, that in fact she had secret powers and was herself my birth control, that things would shrivel in that bed of hers, or under her gaze. I thought of the princess who had a pea in the mattress that only she could feel, but unlike in the fairytale, I had put it there myself. Because I was cunning enough to conceal something so tiny yet enormous, I felt a strange surge of power.

It was too late to tell Ray, I decided. I had been a few paragraphs, at the most, in his life story. He could not sort it out with me, because it had got to the stage where he had no say in your arrival. You were a certainty. Also, if Ray knew, he would get his parents involved. Then what? I'd derail their junior José Rizal. And how would I find him in Adelaide, even if I wanted to?

"I'll tell you what," your Grand Mar bargained. "You can keep this baby if you become its sister."

I thought she had truly gone nuts. "How can I be its sister when I'm going to be the one giving birth?" I demanded.

"Sure, you push the baby out, but after that, then what? Who's going to look after it?"

"I'll look after *my* baby."

"Ha! What do you think you'll give birth to? A plastic blinking-drinking-peeing doll? Do you think it's that simple to look after an infant? If we tell the baby that you're their sister, they'll never know any better, and you won't have the responsibility and pressure of bringing them up."

"You can't just take my baby from me."

"I'm not taking anything away from you – we'll all be living in the same house. If you can't bring up a kid, you'll have to put it up for adoption. If you have no support, if you look like the sixteen-year-old imbecile that you are, see how many people will allow you to raise a child!"

"That's because you won't let me do *anything* by myself!"

"Who got themselves into this mess in the first place? As if you could look after a baby. Ha, you who can't even look after yourself."

"You just want to take every good thing I have away from me!"

"How is this a good thing, huh? I'm making a big sacrifice for you here," sighed your Grand Mar. "Do you think I want to be a mother again at the age of forty? Life is hard enough already without this."

"Then don't do it," I told her. "You're always doing things for me and then hating it, and then blaming me."

"Who's the father then, eh? If you find that deadhead boy who got you like this and make him take some responsibility, then I'll start treating you like an adult. But until then, you can't be trusted with anything. You're sly and secretive; how can anyone even trust you with a baby?"

So this was my punishment for not telling her things. She was going to make you hers.

"The baby can call me Mar," she declared, which in our medieval language could either mean grandma or mother, depending on which tone you used; and did not sound that different from mama or mum.

"No."

"You'll go back to school," she continued. "You think I had the luxury of school when I was your age? You can still have a decent life."

"No!"

I didn't care about school, or the rest of my life. I couldn't imagine a day of your existence where I would not feel murderous rage that your Grand Mar had taken you over and bossed us both around, dolled you up in her stupid outfits and tried to make you a better version of me, hoping that this time things would work out and you would make her proud by being the ideal girl. I wondered whether you would have a better life if we adopted you out.

Although she expected absolute honesty from me, your Grand Mar lied to me every day, in small and big ways. As a kid I had been too gullible to know any better. "There's no chocolate in the house," she'd say, straight-faced. "People will only love you if you are clean and pretty." It was her way of controlling me, so

I knew it would be unblinkingly easy for her to lie to you too. But this was the biggest lie of them all, and she'd be forcing me to maintain it forever.

"No!" I repeated.

I thought of the day I went to watch *Labyrinth*. I thought about the innocence of that girl, the one who'd been so smitten by the Goblin King's charms that she had completely failed to notice the most disturbing aspect of his character: that Jareth is a literal cradle-snatcher. He steals Sarah's baby brother and tells her to fear him, love him and obey him, and he will be her slave. But it's all a lie. He never intends to give the baby back – he intends to keep Sarah in the Underground world with him. "It's only forever," he tells her, "not long at all."

I couldn't imagine lying to you my whole life.

Chapter 7

While you were inside me, I thought, you were still safe. You were still *mine*. You would go wherever I went. You would eat whatever I ate. I could at least take care of you that way.

A few days later, Dr Masano called me with the results of my blood tests. She told me that I was lacking in certain vitamins and minerals.

"We need to go to the chemist," I told your Grand Mar. "The doctor said I'm low in iron and vitamin D."

"What does that mean?" she asked.

"I don't know. But we need them for the baby to be healthy."

Your Grand Mar had already started giving me peculiar advice. "Drink lots of milk so the baby will have white skin. No coffee or chocolate unless you want the baby to be dark. Eat peanuts so your milk will come when it's time." Until now, I'd never even thought of my body as a feeding machine. Gross.

"These Western doctors don't know anything," she scoffed. "Did you see how young she looked? I guarantee you she hasn't had a baby. What they learn is only what they read from books. She just wants to fill you up with pills you don't need. She probably gets a cut from the pharmacy."

"But they're vitamins," I protested. "You don't need a prescription to get them. They're off the shelf. And she said I need them."

"Nonsense. You just need to eat well. I never took any vitamin crap when I was pregnant with you and you turned out healthy. I'm going to make you lots of herbal soups. That's all you need."

I called up the clinic the next day when your Grand Mar had gone to work. "My mother won't get me the vitamins," I told Dr Masano.

"Is it the cost? Do you have a healthcare card?" she asked.

"No, I'm sorry, Dr Masano, you don't get it. She thinks that I shouldn't be taking any pills."

There was a pause. I thought I heard the doctor mutter something under her breath.

"She thinks I can just get them from food," I explained, "so I called to ask if you can tell me what food I should be eating to get vitamin D and iron."

"For iron – leafy greens like spinach. Pumpkin seeds. Beef. Sardines. Oat bran. For vitamin D, make sure you spend some time in the sun every day."

Before she hung up, Dr Masano said, "You call me any time, Karuna, if you have any more questions like this. I'll get Kathy from reception to put you through if I'm not too busy, or I'll call you back. I admire your perseverance. You know how to look after yourself."

"No, I don't," I replied. "That's why I called you. I just want my baby to be okay."

True to her word, your Grand Mar made me lots of herbal soups with weird combinations of ingredients: red dates and fish, pork bones and lotus roots. When we next went grocery

shopping, I put pumpkin seeds, sardines and spinach in our trolley. She took out the sardines, but left the spinach and pumpkin
seeds, and that evening, made them into a chicken soup for me,
adding in small dried berries.

I longed for lollies and chocolate. Cherry Ripes, Bounties,
Violet Crumbles, Fruit Tingles, White Knights. I dreamed
about them. I especially hated it when the Cadbury Flake commercial came on. The only sugary snack in our house was a box
of sultanas so old that they were covered in a white powder, and
each sultana looked like a desiccated spider stomach. I didn't
dare touch them.

"It's going to be a girl," your Grand Mar told me when she
discovered my cravings, but she still didn't buy me any sweets.
Already, she was determining what you would be made of –
more snakes and snails and puppy dogs' tails, I thought, than
sugar and spice and everything nice.

I turned up at my new school so infrequently they could barely
keep track of me. They didn't know I was pregnant. I think they
tried calling our house a couple of times, when your Grand Mar
was at work and I was home, but I never picked up the phone.
I just stayed in, sniffing whiteboard markers, painting my nails
and reading. Your Grand Mar didn't suspect I wasn't going,
especially when I'd ask her to drive me twenty minutes to the
library every Saturday to borrow my week's supply of books.

"Good thing you are working twice as hard at school," your
Grand Mar muttered, "because by the fifth month you won't be
able to concentrate. Your brain will turn to congee."

She didn't know that the books I borrowed were large-print novels that looked like textbooks with their plain covers. I read Sally Beauman, Tom Clancy, Anne Tyler, Nevil Shute: it didn't matter to me. I knew I could have borrowed guides to pregnancy but I was too scared to want to know exactly what was going on inside my body.

One morning, I couldn't stand the boredom. There was only so much reading you could do before you felt like just a pair of eyes attached to a nauseous digestive tract. There were only so many herbal soups you could drink. I'd devoured my latest stash of books, and there was nothing good to eat at home.

I trudged downstairs and around the corner. Sammy's Milk Bar had been there for at least twenty years. On the wall you could even see the faint traces of an Uncle Toby's Oats advertisement painted over in cream. Mrs Allen was there, behind the counter, enslaved by her two-cent Mates and one-cent Buddies, Freckles and aniseed rings. They were on low shelves in a glass cabinet, so that any six-year-old with twenty cents could make her crawl on hand and knee to gather their carefully considered confectionery.

By the corner was a swivel stand that held pre-packaged lollies. While she was busy with a stampede of schoolkids, I stuffed one of those bags inside your Grand Par's loose flannel shirt and walked out. Allen's Strawberries and Cream. They even had her name on them! The dusty packet was her property, and I had pilfered it. It had been too easy. I really was invisible, I thought. People had stopped seeing me. Maybe I was only visible to your Grand Mar.

Back upstairs, I barely looked at each soft white disc with the glowing red globule in the middle. I just chewed and chewed like a demented cow. I scoffed the whole bag in less than ten minutes. They made me incredibly thirsty, so I had to drink two glasses of water as well.

I stood over the sink with immediate regrets, trying not to see the mould clustered at the base of the tap.

Then I hurled everything back up.

The liquidy mess looked like a mixture of blood and bone, like some horrible botched abortion. Turning the tap on full blast, I tried to rinse it all down the sink, but the unchewed bits clogged up the plughole and I had to poke them down with a chopstick.

I went into the bathroom and wiped the tears and snot and sour spit from my face. Unable to look at myself in the mirror, I imagined what Ray would think of me now. Fucking idiot, I thought, he got me this way. I couldn't stand being in the flat any longer – it reeked of vomit – so I locked the door and went outside again.

Somehow, I ended up at the community centre. I knew, deep down, that Ray wouldn't be there, that he'd left for Adelaide. But like one of those toy cars that has to be dragged backwards before it can propel itself forwards, I went back. What trace of him did I expect to find? A secret letter hidden in the *Free Books* box? The box was still there, but now it was on a trestle table in the hallway. Most of the crappy books were still in it. For the first time, I noticed that the surnames of the authors on the spines all began with W. I wondered where the rest of the letters were. Flicking through the spines slowly, I hoped against hope that Ray had stashed a little note for me. Near the end, I wanted to hurl that stupid box against the wall and break a window, and I might have if I hadn't been interrupted.

"Excuse me, can I help you?"

A man in a navy short-sleeved shirt peered down the corridor, pushing his mop and bucket in front of him like a gammy leg.

"I'm just getting a free book," I said, and grabbed one at random. Then I marched out of the community centre like I was on some kind of mission, even though I knew I belonged nowhere and to no one, and no public place wanted me.

The flat still smelled like sick when I returned. I looked at the book in my hands. Just my luck, I thought. Instead of a novel I'd picked up another book of poetry, this time a Best Of collection by someone named Judith Wright. Looking through the contents I saw a lot of poems with "Woman" in their title: "Woman to Man", "Woman to Child", "Woman's Song". Sappy love ballads, I thought. Ick. But I also found a poem I liked called "The Killer", about a snake getting killed and ants infesting its eyeballs, and one about a trapped dingo.

Then I came across one about "the eyeless labourer in the night", a "selfless, shapeless seed" building for its "resurrection day". It scared the bejesus out of me because I knew exactly what she was on about. Now I knew I had no control over my body. I could find myself hurling into a public rubbish bin. I could pee in the middle of the market. You, a blameless but selfish parasite, were sucking the life out of me.

First my body had belonged to your Grand Mar, and now it belonged to you. And soon, you would belong to your Grand Mar and not me. Nothing was fair, I thought. I couldn't even keep a packet of lollies inside myself. How was I meant to keep you safe?

*

I'd got so used to feeling vomity all the time that the morning I woke up without nausea I thought I had lost you, or never had you. I actually felt good. Then guilty. Then, heaving with panic, I called Dr Masano. When I finally got through, I told her, "I think I've just lost the baby. I don't feel sick anymore."

"Congratulations," she said, "you've just lost your nausea. You're going to be feeling great in the next few days."

And she was right! The next day, I felt so good that I decided to pay Tweezer a little visit at Christ Our Saviour College. I stole a dollar from your Grand Mar's purse before she left for work, and took a bus. I had timed my arrival for when the girls would be out for lunch so I could catch Tweezer by the gate and tell her. I looked out the bus window as my old world came back into focus – the factory roofs zig-zagging like giant saw teeth sliding across the sky, their tessellated wire fences, the gold tickle of sunlight in the mid-afternoon.

I'd arrived early enough to see the girls emerge from the yellow-brick school building in clusters of two or three, clutching chip packets and pieces of fruit, to claim wooden benches, or patches of concrete if they were slow. I knew where Tweezer would be headed, and soon enough I spotted her, walking with another girl.

"Tweezer!" I yelled, waving like nuts. When she saw me, she started to run. We whooshed together in a massive hug, and I smelled the familiar lemony smell of her shampoo.

"This is Adisa," Tweezer said, when we finally parted.

Her friend had dark eyebrows, enormous green eyes that slanted upwards like a cat's, and hair cut into a short bob. She looked like she belonged in a 1920s silent film.

"Hello," I said.

Adisa gave me a wide smile and said, "Hello, Karuna."
I hated her straightaway, because she knew my name. It meant
that Tweezer had talked about me, but Adisa had no right to
think that she and I were going to be friends.

I sat miserably with them on a bench while Tweezer excit-
edly filled me in on all the things I had missed since the year
began. Adisa constantly interrupted her: "Oh yeah, you have
to tell her how Mr Sloane brought his baby into Maths class,"
and "You have to tell her *why* Debbie and Hanray aren't friends
anymore," and she'd turn to me, her teal eyes shining with
glee. She *wasn't even there* for the development of Debbie and
Hanray's friendship. She'd only just arrived from a school in
Broadmeadows at the beginning of the year, and already she was
acting like she was in and I was out.

It was meant to be just me and Tweezer, but while I had been
missing her like an amputated leg, Tweezer had been moving on.
She glanced between me and Adisa as if she couldn't believe her
luck, having both best friends in one spot. I stayed for another
twenty minutes, then I told them I had to catch my bus and left.

That evening, when your Grand Mar came home from work, she
asked me, "Did you take a dollar from my purse?"

"No."

"Strange," she muttered, "I thought I had an extra dollar in
there. In fact, I was sure . . ."

I wanted to see Tweezer again the next day, but knew I couldn't
steal another cent. I also knew I couldn't go at lunchtime, because

Adisa would be there. So I set out at one-thirty to get to the school before three-thirty. It was only a twenty-minute drive, but took me almost two hours to walk. I knew I had ten or fifteen minutes at most to talk to Tweezer before she would have to go home.

We never called each other on the phone – her parents believed idle chatter was an evil female habit, so I had never got her number. And even if she was allowed to call me, Tweezer would never have any privacy inside that house – their only phone, a beige rotary thing, was in the hallway, sitting on a small table attached to a little chair.

As soon as I reached the school grounds, I plonked myself down on a wooden bench. I was exhausted, but Dr Masano had said exercise was good for me.

Tweezer spotted me. I got up and ran towards her before anyone else could join us. "Tweezer, I need to tell you something important."

"Yes?" Her eyes were bright with excitement.

"I need to tell you alone, right now."

"Umm, okay. But I gotta get home soon . . ."

"I know, I know, so we gotta talk fast. Let's go to the corner near the tennis courts." Without looking back, I headed there, knowing she would follow. Tweezer could not resist a secret.

"I'm having a baby," I blurted when we got to the corner.

The first thing Tweezer did was look at my belly in disbelief – I wasn't fat yet.

"What?"

"I screwed someone over the summer break."

"Who was it?"

"Some guy I met in a tutoring class for dumbarses."

She glanced down and I thought she was looking at my belly again, but then realised she was searching my hands. She was looking to see if I was wearing a ring.

"Are you still with him?"

"What do you think?" I wasn't exactly glowing like the Princess Bride.

"But do you still see him around?"

"No. *He* doesn't even know, to be honest."

Tweezer gaped at me. "Why not?"

"Because he's in Adelaide now." Neither Tweezer or I had ever been to another state, so he might as well have been in a different galaxy.

"Why?" she asked. "Why did you do it?"

I was taken aback. No one else had bothered to ask me that. They'd all just assumed some boy took advantage of me.

"Because I could," I replied truthfully, but the moment those words came out, they sounded wrong – stupidly defiant, like a kid justifying why they'd touched the wet paint when there was clearly a sign on the bench.

"What was his name?"

"Ray."

"Were you in love with him?"

"No."

How could I explain that it was more how he made me feel about myself? Like I was a separate person from my parents. It wouldn't have made sense to Tweezer, who cooked with her mother and served her brother and father first.

"But . . . why?" she repeated, her voice now a whine.

Then I realised Tweezer was scared of me, this grown-up girl

growing a baby. Only a year ago, we had made fun of the popular girls, guessing which one would get knocked up first. How
could she have known it would be me? And if she couldn't have
guessed that I had it in me to do this, what other secrets was
I hiding from her? I'd crossed a line, done something she'd been
planning to do herself, but in a decade's time. And I'd done it in
a way that seemed cheap and quick and easy. Like we were both
planning a feast, saving up our most precious ingredients, but
then I'd gone ahead and eaten a two-minute microwave meal
instead, without telling her.

Tweezer probably thought that my new school had made
me feral. I was tall, much taller than her now. But I was still the
same small person inside. Probably even smaller now than I'd
ever been.

"Are you going to keep the baby or adopt it out?" Tweezer
asked.

"We're going to keep it," I said. "My mum reckons she's
going to look after it so I can go back to school."

"Oh," said Tweezer, suddenly excited. "Are you coming back
here?"

"I wish. But can you imagine the nuns letting someone like
me back in?"

I'd walked almost four hours to see Tweezer for ten minutes, but
the next day I did the same, and the day after that. There was
nothing to do at home. I was out of the house from one-thirty
to five-thirty. Carrying a two-litre bottle of diluted orange juice
with me, I popped into service stations if I needed to pee.

I told Tweezer about the Greek girls at my new school. "They sound awful," she sympathised. I told her about your Grand Mar's ultimatum and how I didn't want to be a sister – "It's not fair, it's *my* baby!" – and she squeezed my hand tightly. But most of all, she wanted to hear about Ray – what he looked like, what he'd said to me and whether he was coming back.

"Tweezer, look at me," I said. "I've felt like chucking up my guts for a whole month. I've peed my pants walking down stairs. I've been stung by Dettol and had needles poked in my arms. This isn't a romantic comedy, and he's not the lead. He's not around, he's dead to me, he's a ghost. This is a bloody horror movie."

On my fourth visit, Tweezer told me, "Hold out your hand. I have a surprise for you." She placed something small, cold and round in my palm.

"What's this?"

"Adisa pinched some money from her mum's purse and got it for you."

The ring was gold and had a diamond in it.

"Oh my God. How much did Adisa pinch from her mum?"

"Don't worry, it came from an egg."

"Huh?"

"One of those plastic eggs you get when you put fifty cents into the vending machine."

"Oh."

I looked at the ring more closely. Because I owned no real jewellery, I couldn't tell a false diamond ring from a real one. Maybe a real one was shinier or heavier or something, but I was still very touched that Adisa, a stranger, a girl I hadn't liked much and showed it, had done this for me. It was more than most adults had done, except Dr Masano, but then, that was her job.

"Tell Adisa thanks."

"Yeah, we don't want people to look down on you," explained Tweezer. "This way they'll think you're engaged to some handsome rich guy."

I wore the ring all the way home, and imagined Ray had got it for me; and that in a few months' time he'd ask me to join him in Adelaide. I thought I looked very respectable and grown-up. Maybe I'd stop wearing your Grand Par's schleppy clothes and start dressing like a future doctor's wife, all blazers, ballet flats and lace blouses.

One day, Mrs Zafeiriou came to collect Tweezer and I knew it was the beginning of the end of my school visits.

She looked at my face, then down to where my dumb decision clotted in my belly. Even though she was standing a good metre away from me, I could smell the cloying scent of cut roses on her, and it was all I could do not to gag. She grabbed Tweezer by the shoulders and marched her away like a prisoner of war, without saying a word.

The next afternoon, Tweezer ran over to me. "Karuna, you can't come here again!" she said. "Spiros is coming to pick me up now. I'm in big trouble for hanging out with you."

Like it was my fault for not only getting myself into trouble, but her as well.

"You're not hanging out with me – we just talk for a few

minutes after school, for God's sake. How did your mum know I was knocked up anyway?"

Tweezer didn't answer me. "I'm sorry. Quick, you have to go, it only takes him seven minutes to walk here from St Andrew's."

Tweezer's brother was made to collect her from school instead of letting her walk the few streets home alone. She was now in the same humiliating category as Ranju, who wore long white trousers beneath her uniform skirt, and whose turbaned brother came to collect her every afternoon.

But I didn't care about the petty sufferings of Tweezer, her witchy mum or dumb-arse brother. All I could think about was her cowardice. I knew I had absolutely no power of my own, but I'd still managed to find ways to make my own decisions – like visiting her. Come to think of it, all she seemed to want from me, from my short visits, was news. She wanted to hear how the baby was growing and what it felt like; and the most outrageous things your Grand Mar would say or do. Then her eyes would widen and she'd shake her head and say, "Wow, I can't imagine." Of course she couldn't. After all, she still worshipped your Grand Mar, and so maybe she thought I was blowing things out of proportion. In fact, compared to her own family, your Grand Mar seemed soft and lenient.

I'd had a little fun, and my fun had created concentric circles of suffering for everyone else, a red boot landing in the middle of an unsuspecting puddle. Well, before I went, I would stomp as hard as I could, make the biggest splash.

"I know you dobbed me into your parents."

"No, I didn't!"

"Then how do they know?"

Tweezer didn't say anything.

"Up yours, Tweezer," I hissed, and walked away.

It was the April school holidays, and one Saturday your Grand Mar wanted me to go down to the milk bar to get more milk. "It's good for the baby," she told me.

"Fine." All I'd been doing that morning was watching the music videos on *Rage* anyway.

"Wait for me to put on my shoes."

"You don't need to come," I said, standing up. "Really." But she was already slipping on her black plastic slippers.

"Don't walk so fast!" she told me when we were outside. "You could trip and fall." She was already treating me like a ninety-year-old woman, so what normally would have been a seven-minute walk ended up taking almost twenty. I would probably have got there faster if I crawled.

The moment we entered, Mrs Allen glared at me from behind the counter and my heart stopped.

"She took a pack of lollies from me."

"Sorry?" Your Grand Mar looked up.

"Your girl stole a packet of lollies from me last month. I recognise her face."

Your Grand Mar turned to me, but I said nothing.

"She came in during the after-school stampede, when I had all those primary-school kids in. I was down low but I saw her through the glass of the cabinet, saw her taking a pack from this rack."

"But how can she get them if they behind you?" your Grand Mar asked.

"Well, after she pinched it I had to move the rack so no other five-finger discounters could get to them, didn't I!"

"I'm very sorry," said your Grand Mar, putting ten dollars down on the glass counter. "Very sorry."

Mrs Allen took the money and shoved it in her paisley-print apron without looking at her. "Next time, I call the cops," she warned.

We didn't get the milk we'd come for.

In our flat, your Grand Mar let rip. "What under heaven have I done to deserve such bad karma?" she screamed. "You don't have to work. You don't have to do the shopping or pay bills. You have a kitchen full of food. You have everything you need here. And you still go out and do this to me! I spend all day at work worrying about what mischief you'll get up to next. It's like you can't help yourself. You were put here to torment me for my sins!"

Chapter 8

Your Grand Mar locked me up the next day.

She left early for work, so I didn't discover I was locked in until around eleven o'clock, when I decided I might as well go downstairs to collect the mail and see if the latest *Reader's Digest* had come. Your Grand Mar had sneakily got me to reroute your Grand Par's subscription to our flat.

The spare key that I'd always left hanging from the hook above our telephone was gone. I wondered whether I had put it somewhere yesterday and forgotten, but I couldn't find it after looking everywhere – in my bag, on tabletops and between sofa cushions, even in the bathroom cabinet. Then I knew that it was deliberate.

Oh well, I thought. It was probably fair punishment for making her fork out ten dollars to Mrs Allen to save her face and my skin. I could wait this out. The least I could do was clean, so I tidied the house. I used vinegar in the bathroom, relined the kitchen drawers with junk-mail advertisements, and even wiped all the sticky bottoms of jam jars and tinned vegetables. When your Grand Mar returned home that night, she said nothing about the state of the house, and I said nothing about her locking me in.

She locked me in the next day as well. I cleaned out the fridge. I sponged down the doors and windows. I even used an old toothbrush to scrub the window jambs.

The day after, I was still locked in. I vacuumed the sofa and curtains. I reorganised our bedsheet and towel cupboard. Then I watched some television. A Shirley Temple movie was on, and I remembered how your Grand Par used to call me his little Chinese Shirley Temple. I hadn't seen him for ages, and often wondered whether he even knew what was happening to me, if your Grand Mar had told him yet. If he knew, he'd help me. He was a fixer, not a whinger, but I had no idea how to contact him.

On the fourth day, I sat in the spare room, sorting through your Grand Par's stuff. She'd taken his *Longman Dictionary of Contemporary English*, all his old magazines and even, saddest of all, a chipped peanut butter jar filled with his greasy pens, freebies from car parts companies. His *Reader's Digest*s went back as far as the mid-1970s, and I wondered if he'd noticed his supply of new issues had been diverted.

When your Grand Mar returned home that evening, I tried to get her to talk to me again. "See here, it says you can win a hundred dollars just by writing in and telling a joke."

"Well, why don't you do it then?" she asked derisively.

"I will," I told her. "I will win us one hundred dollars." It would be easy money. I thought of all the jokes I could make up for the "All in a Day's Work" or "Laughter, the Best Medicine" sections.

So the next day, still locked in, I wrote a joke, and when she returned late at night, I waved my entry at her. "Mah, I need a stamp to post this off."

"What is it?"

"The joke for the magazine I told you about."

"Forget about it," she said. "Look, why don't you enter the free competitions? You can win us a car or a house." She had seen the pictures of prizes to be won. But I knew that you had to buy whatever was on offer inside those envelopes – the *Reader's Digest Household Hints and Handy Tips*, or the *Condensed Jeffrey Archer*. They didn't let you win for nothing. When I was an adult I would be able to buy a thirty-seven-cent stamp. For now I was stuck.

But at least we had reached a truce, your Grand Mar and me – at least she was talking to me again.

Then she noticed my left hand. "What's that on your finger?"

"A ring." I'd put it back on because I hadn't done any heavy-duty cleaning today.

"Where'd you get it?"

"Someone gave it to me," I said mysteriously, smugly.

"Let me have a look!" She grabbed my hand, examined the ring for a few seconds, then dropped my wrist. "Junk," she said. "Take it off."

"No."

"Are you insane? Anyone can see it's a fake. Who'd give you a thousand-dollar ring anyway? You look twelve years old. Cheap rubbish. Where'd he get it from? A vending machine?"

Because nothing that came out of her mouth was kind, because every word was seared on both sides with sarcasm, and because I didn't have any other new thoughts to fill my mind during the day, your Grand Mar's scorn bubbled into a terrible stew inside me. I threw the ring at her.

"Dad would never let you lock me up like this!" I yelled. "You take everything that's good from me. It's your fault he left us."

Surprisingly, she was deadly calm. "Ha, you're still stuck on your useless dad. Has he tried to contact you during all this time? I tell him that maybe he might want to call on his daughter every now and then to check that she's still alive. But has he called? Have you heard from him?"

I didn't say anything. Ever since we'd moved to the flat, I thought your Grand Mar had been blocking your Grand Par from finding me. Never had I considered that he just wouldn't make the effort. I didn't know what to think or believe.

"I bet you didn't even tell him where we live, or give him our new number," I said uncertainly.

"Why would I lie to you?" she demanded.

"You lie to me all the time."

"I'm telling the truth."

"Fine, then. Give me his new phone number and I'll call him."

"Over your Mah's dead body!" she retorted. "You don't want to seek him out if he doesn't give a shit about you. I don't want a daughter of mine to learn she has to chase useless men down, only to be hurt a hundred times worse."

Just because he doesn't love you, I thought, doesn't mean he doesn't love me. I didn't say this, of course. I was not like your Grand Mar. I didn't hurl terrible truths at people I loved.

On the seventh day, I told her I needed to go back to school. The Easter break had almost ended.

"When you've been staying away on and off all those months and pretending to go? Don't lie to me now. It was probably one of those feral state-school boys who got you this way. Am I right? I bet they gave you that tacky ring."

I said nothing.

"If you had hung around some good Asian girls, none of this would have happened. Those girls have their heads screwed on right, they go home every afternoon and don't loiter, they do their homework and study and concentrate on getting smarter. And why didn't you go to the free tutoring program like I told you to?"

I hesitated. "I went once, but it was for little kids."

"Who was it?" She went off again, like a wound-up yapping toy that could not be stopped, and I made my eyes vague and my mouth a straight line like on a life-support machine, not emitting any beeps, forever holding my peace.

"It's that Tweezer," your Grand Mar shouted. "She and that brother of hers. I bet it was one of his friends!"

I kept my mouth closed, in case I laughed out loud. Even though he was tall, Spiros was only thirteen.

"Aha! I'm right, aren't I?"

I didn't reply. Instead, I said levelly, "The government will be onto us if you don't let me go back to school."

"As if I'm the one stopping you! As if it's me keeping your lazy arse around the house all day watching television and eating. What's the point?" she screeched. "What's the point of you doing nothing all day while I work to death? I don't know what sins I've committed to be so cursed. You've cursed my life."

"I need to go back to school," I repeated.

"How do I know where you go each day and what you do?" she yelled. "I don't know you anymore!"

Of course not.

Finally, just when I thought she would relent, when I saw her shoulders sag and a sigh leak out, she turned to me and said, "What's the use of going back to school when you'll just have to leave again in a few months' time?"

Why didn't I run away? The truth was, I wasn't so much scared as exhausted. I simply had no energy left to fight harder. It was like the fairy-witch putting a spell on Sleeping Beauty. Except Sleeping Beauty could rely on her looks for her revival, whereas I was more Sleeping Ugly, my mouth dry and open, lips peeling like sunburn. Whenever I woke up from one of my restless naps, I felt worse than before, dopey, oily-haired, puffy-faced, elephant-heavy. What kind of prince would bother reviving such a monster?

Where would I go anyway?

On Monday, I woke up before your Grand Mar and made toast with kaya jam. By the time she was up, I was already dressed, drinking instant coffee with sweetened condensed milk, my schoolbag at my feet.

Your Grand Mar didn't say anything, but when she left for work, she put the spare key on the kitchen bench.

Walking down the stairs, I felt like someone had connected my nostrils up with a tube while I was asleep and pumped water into me. My fingers and toes were liquid-filled rubber gloves.

Outside, I remembered a nursery rhyme we used to sing when we walked down pavements. *Don't step on cracks, you'll break your mother's back. Don't step on stones, you'll break your mother's bones*. I wibble-wobbled on the footpath and smelled wattle. The sky was too bright. The seasons had changed without me being there, and a thought blipped across my mind – that winter would turn into spring even if I wasn't here, that life was going on within me but it would also go on without me. I was a carrier, a shell, a cocoon, but once you emerged, I could be discarded. I knew these were bad thoughts. I did not stop them, though, because they were the only thoughts I had to call my own.

"You'll always be welcome here," I remembered Mrs Stubinger, the principal of Christ Our Saviour, telling me before I left. "You don't need to be a stranger." I walked faster. The street was like a movie set where the actors had all gone back to their real lives, after trashing the scenery at a giant end-of-shoot party. I saw an ice-cream wrapper on the pavement, among a million cigarette stubs, little fires put out after lighting up the chimneys of a thousand lungs. Green glints of broken bottles. The paper tongue of a discarded party whistle.

A car drove by and slowed down. One of those vehicles whacked together from two separate junkyard ones, the front brown, the back blue. A head stuck itself out of the driver's seat window, all jagged teeth and craggy cheeks. "I don't pay taxes just so youse fucking reffos can breed like animals!"

I kept moving. Soon I was at the big white cross outside the small chapel of Christ Our Saviour College. The green and white plastic sign screwed into the brick next to the office door saying *Neighbourhood Watch Area*. The yellow sign saying *Safety House Zone*.

All three hundred and fifty-two girls were in class, and the place looked deserted. I expected surreal things to happen.

I wondered where that bitch Tweezer was, and what she was doing. Despite my rage, I found myself thinking of her often. Too late, I realised she'd been my one true friend.

The school was cleaner than the outside world. The only rubbish on the floor was a single serviette, like the decomposing corpse of an origami bird.

I pushed open the glass door leading to reception.

Mrs Natale behind the desk looked up, saw me and smiled. Then she saw my bump. Her eyebrows stretched to line up with the top frame of her glasses.

"Karuna, what are you doing here?" she asked.

"Help," I exhaled, because suddenly I felt doggone exhausted. "Help me, please, Mrs Natale. I am stuck. I need to see Mrs Stubinger."

I started to cry. I couldn't help it.

Mrs Natale stood up. "Don't worry, love. Take it easy. Take a seat. I'll find out if she's available right now."

I sat myself on the soft, rose-coloured sofa for visitors. I looked at the modest glass awards cabinet by the reception desk, at the Red Cross Appeal trophy. On the wall was a photograph of four girls who had excelled in Year 12 last year.

Mrs Natale offered to take me to the meeting room, probably because she didn't want me at reception.

A few minutes later, Mrs Stubinger entered.

"I'm having a baby," I blurted out as soon as she sat down.

"Does your current school know about this?" Mrs Stubinger asked gently.

"No, they don't care. I've been away so much this year."

"Do your parents know?"

"My mum does."

I wanted to tell her everything – the bone-deep loneliness of being locked in at home, the loss of Tweezer and the feeling of drowning in my own crazy brain.

"Poor, dear thing," she cooed at me. "You look so tired."

I sniffed.

"Perhaps you need to go home and rest. Does your mother know you're here?"

I shook my head. I thought Mrs Stubinger would be able to help, but here she was, trying to fob me off.

"Help me," I begged, "help me! Take me away. I'll even go to live with the nuns!"

Mrs Stubinger looked at me with her understanding eyes. "Listen, Karuna, things aren't done that way anymore. And for the better, too."

"But when my baby comes, my mum is going to take it!"

"Take it where?"

"Just take it, look after it, make it her own baby." I knew how I sounded the moment those words came out: like a child railing over a confiscated birthday toy she was too young to play with.

"You know, Karuna, the nuns used to take babies too, but they took them away and the young new mothers never saw them again. Your mother is probably doing what's right for both of you." She paused. "Does your mum hit you?"

"No."

"Is it just you and your mum living at home?"

"Yes."

"Do you see much of your father?"

"He moved out."

"Do you have a stepdad?"

"No."

"So your mother is your legal guardian?"

"Yes."

"Sweetie, we have to let her know that you're here with us."

I cried some more. But in the end, I had to give in. I had no more energy to speak, let alone fight with someone who'd only offer wordy compassion but return me to the flat. I gave Mrs Stubinger the phone number for Mrs Osman's salon.

During the forty-minute wait for your Grand Mar to arrive, Mrs Stubinger made me a cup of Milo and opened up a packet of Mint Slices. She asked the librarian, Mrs Burgess, to bring me a stack of discontinued books from the library so I would have something to read, and sent for a salad sandwich from the canteen for my journey back. And because she did all these fairy-godmother things for me, the gap between what I fantasised she could do and what she was actually doing widened until I was angry at her for not doing more. But she just sat there chatting about how it must be an exciting time for me.

She even brought in a translator. Mrs Ling taught Year Eight Maths but I had never had her as a teacher – she was straight-as-a-ruler strict. Her fringe was so even that the top third of her head looked like it had been sliced off when she sat in front of a blackboard. She had on a pleated green skirt and a matching blouse with a bow on the collar and plastic buttons with gold edges.

Your Grand Mar arrived in her shining black slacks and a regal-purple woollen cardigan with silver sequins and silver piping. I saw Mrs Ling noticing your Grand Mar's thick hair, her unlined skin, her pencilled-in arched brows and bur-gundy lipstick. The two thick gold chains around her neck and jade bracelet around her wrist. Your Grand Mar didn't look like a slacker, lazy-arse mum. Your Grand Mar looked like a grand dame, a dignified woman who took care of herself. Your Grand Mar smiled at Mrs Ling, a smile like she had lollies in her hand-bag for every child in the school.

Then Mrs Ling looked at me – unwashed hair like an oil spill down the polyester grey sweatshirt covering my shoulders, jeans stiff with crap from cleaning the shower-grout, belly big with you and face like a rubber mask.

Your Grand Mar and Mrs Ling talked to each other in Mandarin. I couldn't understand anything.

"She's okay," Mrs Ling told Mrs Stubinger in English. "Her mother is looking after her."

I couldn't believe it! Mrs Ling didn't see how sick I was. She couldn't see that I was now just a flaking cocoon.

"I've been at home for two weeks, I haven't even been allowed to go anywhere except to hang out the clothes on the rooftop of our block of flats!"

"You could get cold and sick. The worst thing is to be sick when you are giving birth," your Grand Mar said calmly, looking directly at Mrs Ling.

"Your mother's just making sure you get plenty of rest," Mrs Ling said to me, and then she turned back to your Grand Mar. "You should go on walks through the neighbourhood with her. Let her get some fresh air now that spring is here."

"Sister, I go with her to every hospital appointment," your Grand Mar replied. "But we will go on walks together. Yes."

It seemed crazy how this was happening, how if you scrubbed up well, you could cover all your tracks. But I would not let it go. I wanted to drag them back to me. I couldn't do it if I kept snivelling, but I couldn't stop either. Soon the hiccups came. I didn't have a tissue, so I used my sleeve. Mrs Ling opened up her handbag and took out a tissue – the expensive, perfumed sort that came in little packets of ten. She was smiling but I noticed she was holding only one corner of the tissue when she passed it to me, like she was scared of catching my misery.

I wiped my nose and said, "Mrs Stubinger, I want to go back to school."

"She go to school," your Grand Mar said coldly. "She go to Corindirk High School."

"But I want to come back here!"

Your Grand Mar glared at me, but I ignored her, appealing straight to Mrs Stubinger. "I know I was just average, but I'll try harder. Please!"

"Here at Christ Our Saviour, we respect different cultural practices," Mrs Stubinger replied kindly. "Sometimes you have to do what doesn't feel comfortable, but will be good for you in the long term. Your mum is just trying to protect you and look after your health. She obviously cares about you very much."

They did not understand how my world had shrunk. They couldn't see that the bigger I got, the smaller I became, and they didn't understand that once the baby came, I would be gone! They just let your Grand Mar take me home. Mrs Stubinger even accompanied us to the bus stop, but I bet she only did it to make sure I would never come back again.

*

"What did you tell the Ghosts?" your Grand Mar demanded when we got home.

"Nothing."

"Don't lie! Got me out of work for this! What a trouble-maker. What sins did I do in my past life to have a daughter like you? Oh Buddha, have mercy on my soul."

She wasn't going to get paid that day because three custom-ers had come into the shop for their appointments and were pissed off she wasn't there. Bad for business, said Mrs Osman. Unreliable.

"Do you know what a stupid thing you did? They could take the baby away! This just proves that there is no way in hell you can look after this child. You keep pulling dangerous stunts like this on me."

Your Grand Mar made me kneel in front of the bright red altar that now sat in our lounge room, the same shrine my friend had knocked over on my eighth birthday. She started chanting, her eyes closed. Forehead to the ground, and then up in a kneel-ing position again. "Buddhas, have mercy on us!" she wailed.

No big, fat, laughing Buddha with babies rolling all over his tummy for your Grand Mar; her gods were punitive ones, red-faced, angry, vindictive. Even the Goddess of Mercy had no mercy. There was a hole at her base and when you looked inside it you could see she was dark and hollow. Her sly brushstroke eyes had the look of a girl who knew she was beautiful because she had been told that her whole life, and she held a drooping green stalk in two sharp fingers like a posh woman with a dirty dishcloth.

Up and down and up and down she went, your Grand Mar. Knees and forehead on the ground, then back on her toes.

It was the "Heads, Shoulders, Knees and Toes" song gone mad. "Name oni tor hooc," she chanted in her corrupted Pali. What did she expect would happen? I wondered. That the Heavens would open up and swallow me whole? That her gods would reverse time?

I realised that even if your Grand Mar had not given your Grand Par our new address, if he had really wanted to find me, he would have. So I knew that the one person who might have been able to help me didn't give a shit.

I stopped praying, because I knew there was no one who could answer my prayers.

Chapter 9

I've found a solution!"

The next day your Grand Mar returned from Mrs Osman's salon exuberant, like she was a gleeful housewife in a cleaning ad and I was a really tough stain.

"That old horse took a lot of convincing, so you'd better not mess up," she said. "Consider yourself very lucky. You are getting this training for free. Other girls have to go to trades college. They have to spend money on useless things like textbooks and sit in class listening to a teacher drone on about cutting fringes. She's even going to pay you to be her apprentice."

Turns out, Mrs Osman would pay me five dollars a day. "We'll need every cent we can get," your Grand Mar said. "Soon there will be three mouths to feed in this household."

I hated going to the salon, but I desperately needed to be out of the house because I was starting to lose the outer edges of my vision. I was worried I'd eventually go blind, like when you turn off a really old television and there's just a speck left in the middle of all that darkness before everything disappears. So I went along with your Grand Mar's plan.

When I got the job with Mrs Osman, no one told me *congratulations, you are now a working woman*; when they looked at my belly they never congratulated me. It was more like, *child, what are you doing, growing like an adult*? When children have children, it freaks people out.

Mrs Osman's salon smelled sweet because of the hot sugar wax she always had boiling on a stove. She had named her business *Caramel* because of that, but I knew that the *Women's Weekly* caramel recipe had butter in it. Hers was just cheap vinegar toffee.

"All the people naming their shops Athena Beauty or Zainab Salon, after themselves! What wankers," she told me. "As if they movie stars. *Caramel* is a good name to remember, a good smell. Even the Australians like to come in here."

Mrs Osman dyed her hair a honey-brown to match, but she didn't bother with her eyebrows, which remained black. She dressed like an elegant liquorice allsort, lots of black broken by bands of pink, green or blue in the form of scarf, belt, shoes. Her deep-set black eyes were framed by cow-length lashes. I had no idea whether she was a lot older or a lot younger than your Grand Mar.

She gave me a big black apron, which covered me from shoulder to knee, and my first tasks were to sweep the hair from the floor after every haircut and tidy up the hairdressing caddies. I swept for a week and thought about Rapunzel. "If you save the long bits of hair, we can sell them to people who make wigs," I suggested.

"No one want black hair," Mrs Osman declared. "Black hair everywhere! No value. They want the gold hair, but how many gold-hair girls we get? Look down and see yourself."

It was true. Most of the hair was black or dark brown, or black with red highlights. If we had any blonde hair, it was usually dyed and brittle, with dark roots. I remembered the fairytale "Cat-Skin", about a king whose dying wife made him promise to only remarry if he could find a woman as fair and golden-haired as she was, so he could only think of marrying his own daughter. Women would come in with pictures cut out from *Woman's Day* – Madonna, Michelle Pfeiffer, Kim Basinger – actresses and singers whose hair colour or texture didn't match their own, asking for the exact same style. Women wanted manes like lions, while men wanted coifs like wildebeest or gelada baboons, those monkeys with the exposed valentine's hearts on their chests. While they waited on Mrs Osman's plastic chairs, the customers would groom themselves like animals in public view, gazing at their reflections on her wall mirrors, chewing on their nails, smelling their hands, sucking their teeth.

"Did ya get your hair cut or not?" blokes would ask when they came to pick up their girlfriends or wives. It confirmed for me something I had long suspected: boys focused on the whole package, not the petty details. They really didn't care about freckles, teeth that were a little large, limbs longer than usual. Only women fussed over the small stuff, and places like Mrs Osman's salon were created for these little flourishes – the tweak of the brow, the smooth lip. You could pull out your own upper-lip hair; you could scrape the hair off your own legs. You didn't need to go to a beauty parlour, but you went there anyway, to see what other women were doing to themselves, how they were making themselves attractive and hear about for whom, and determine whether they were worth it.

"No smile, no beauty face," Mrs Osman always told me, but once I also heard her say to a severe-looking older customer,

"Smiling too much make wrinkle on your eyes." She and your Grand Mar were exactly alike, I thought. They even made the same snide comments about their customers. But when the customers talked, Mrs Osman and your Grand Mar listened as if the women in the chair were their own mother, sister or daughter.

"She wouldn't let me see my own grandchildren!" railed a Greek woman with a fluffy black cloud of hair that Mrs Osman was shaping into a sort of crunchy pith helmet. "Can you believe such a bitch? I tell him not to marry a Russian, they have no family values, the communism screw up their hearts."

"Oh, I know," Mrs Osman sympathised, "I know about terrible in-laws. Before I marry Gregorie, his sister seem so sweet, a primary-school teacher. Who know she would be a crazy nut? She would not let us name our dog Raf because she tell us Rafael will be name of their future child. Even today I don't know when this baby will come!"

Other times, intense and horrible stories would erupt from the small talk like alien eggs hatching when you least expected. "And I said to him, if you love me, why you bring your friends back to rape me?" Mrs Clara-Maria, a thirty-something lady, suddenly asked your Grand Mar, who was massaging perm chemicals into her hair and coiling it into small rollers.

Ten minutes earlier, during the haircut, Mrs Clara-Maria and your Grand Mar had been talking about the *binukot* women of the Philippines – how in the old days, a certain tribe would keep a girl from the age of three away from public view and out of the sun. She could only bathe at night so no one could see her. Then she would be married at thirteen or fourteen, fetching a very good dowry. They were discussing how the preferred looks of a *binukot* – white skin, fragility – were fortunately not the looks that the White Ghosts were after in Asian women, how they liked them the way they liked their bread – baked brown and peasanty.

"Those White Ghost," shouted your Grand Mar, "they so filthy. I know – I was marry to one too. He was not bad as yours, but he have busy eye. Soon he start see difference between me and true Filipino girls with American-sounding voice, and that was the end. Copy of me everywhere, but better, younger."

I couldn't believe your Grand Mar was comparing my father with Mrs Clara-Maria's animal husband.

As I swept the hair from beneath their feet, they both turned and looked at me, Mrs Clara-Maria raising one eyebrow at your Grand Mar. Such bitches, I thought, and threw down my broom and dustpan.

"Ay, ay, ay!" barked your Grand Mar, but I ignored her and went into the small storeroom at the back.

Filthy, your Grand Mar had said, which meant that I was at least fifty per cent filth as well, which was presumably why I'd gotten myself into this mess. I couldn't help it – it was in my genes.

Mrs Osman was sitting on a plastic stool, eating pizza. It wasn't time for my break, so I busied myself tidying the bench-top, stirring the sugar wax and sponging down the sink.

"Would you like some?" she asked, offering me the hot contents of her cardboard box.

Before I could answer, your Grand Mar barged in, still reeking of chemicals. "She can't eat that. It have pineapple."

"So?"

"Pineapple can make you lose baby," your Grand Mar explained.

"That's crazy," said Mrs Osman.

"Is true."

"Did you see it on the news?" Mrs Osman asked. She and your Grand Mar had some kind of obsession with watching the news, because they thought it made them sound educated when they talked to customers. They loved stories of gangs, jealous lovers murdering their women, abducted children and health scares.

"No, is tradition."

"Huh," scoffed Mrs Osman. She glanced at me and winked.

I didn't tell her that your Grand Mar also wanted me to eat a nest made from the saliva of small birds, but fortunately for me she couldn't find that particular delicacy in the Asian grocery stores.

Then she turned to your Grand Mar. "You better check Mrs Clara-Maria's perm is not burn for too long. You don't want her look like a clown."

After your Grand Mar left, Mrs Osman offered me her box again. "Quick, get this into you before your crazy mother come back."

Your Grand Mar once asked Mrs Osman why she didn't do nails. "Can you see me bend down on my hands and knees at the feet of rich housewifes, cleaning their toenails?" she replied. "Head is far as I will go, unless they are lying down on the waxing bed."

Your Grand Mar suggested that Mrs Osman use cotton string to remove customers' unwanted hair to free up the waxing bed on busier days.

"Who use cotton thread to pull out eyebrows here?" cried Mrs Osman. "That's what gypsies do in Egypt. People here want my honey wax. They want to know they so rich they can waste sugar on their legs."

"A roll of cotton costs me twenty cents. I can do a thousand eyebrows with it," muttered your Grand Mar when we got home. "A vat of homemade wax costs her three dollars and lasts only a few days. That woman doesn't know how to run a business."

Your Grand Mar knew that if she ran the salon, she would be able to make it more profitable. She constantly dug for ways to remind Mrs Osman that she'd been a businessowner too. "I telling one customer that after facial peel, she should moisturise her skin and keep out of sun," she told Mrs Osman one day. "Then the skin will grow back soft as baby's. But two day later, she go to the Gold Coast without telling me!"

"Oh God! The humid! The steam!"

"And when she come back, her skin is pink as baby gums, all peeling off."

They envied women who went on holidays so much, women whose husbands earned enough that they didn't have to work. "Those always the ones complaining about how busy they are all the time," sneered your Grand Mar. Your Grand Mar and Mrs Osman lived and prayed to be busy, because more business meant more money.

"They always telling us this is the lucky country," sighed Mrs Osman, "from the moment we arrive. And it's true. We can see that everything is cleaner, healthier, richer, bigger, nicer. But after while, we realise that we are the poorest one in this country, that we are not so lucky after all. We work and work and work, and we are still not as lucky as those born here. No one listen to us. No one care for us when we are old. How they show they appreciate us is they buy our cheap food and service. We stop providing, they stop wanting us. They want us gone."

During one quiet afternoon, they left me alone for an hour and returned, faces flushed with triumph, carrying three over-stuffed plastic bags from the Brotherhood of St Laurence. A dress with a smocked collar. A pale-blue denim overall frock. A grey cotton gown with three-quarter sleeves. They looked like the clothes of a giant toddler girl. "Princess Diana wore the same clothes when she was pregnant," your Grand Mar told me. No, she didn't, I thought. She did not scrounge the second-hand bins for her maternity wear.

"You can't dress like boy all the time, darling," said Mrs Osman. "Waste of that lovely face."

"Yes, this one pay no attention to look good," complained your Grand Mar. "In Philippine every girl care about look good. We the first country in Asia to have two Miss Universe winner." The Miss Universe pageant had been a big deal in our house every year. It was the one time your Grand Mar hadn't minded your Grand Par looking at other women. She would even ask him, "What you think of Miss Australia? Teeth too big?" or "You think Miss Philippine this year look like our Karuna?"

"I remember being young girl," your Grand Mar told Mrs Osman, "when we won our second crown. Her name was Margie, and the judge ask her what she would do with a million dollar. She said she would buy house and land for her family, because those are things she cannot afford." Your Grand Mar sighed and said no more. I knew she was thinking about how we'd once owned a house too, but unlike Margarita Moran I'd now never be her ticket to redeeming this lost concrete glory.

One afternoon, I walked to the discount shop to buy cheap saucepans because Mrs Osman kept burning through them when she made her sugar wax. Your Grand Mar insisted on coming with me to help carry them back.

"Sister! Sister!" came a voice from behind us. It was Aunt Yenny, tugging a cloth-covered shopping trolley. When she got to your Grand Mar, she latched onto her arm like they were real sisters instead of employer and cash-in-hand employee.

"We ran out of bananas at the restaurant. I needed to get some more on sale at Safeway for tonight. You know how those Ghosts love them deep-fried and all flamed up."

It was then that she noticed my belly. "Wah! You have a grandchild coming, sister?"

No, I wanted to say, your restaurant's crappy food made me fat.

Your Grand Mar just smiled like her lips needed a painful stretch.

"Wah. How lucky!" exclaimed Yenny, when the three of us knew she was thinking the opposite. She extended a ringed hand and patted my stomach. "It must be a girl, look how low it's sitting!" Then she turned to my Grand Mar. "Ay, why didn't you invite me to the wedding?"

"What wedding?" wailed your Grand Mar. "There was no wedding."

"Yes," winked Aunt Yenny. "But there will be soon, eh?"

Your Grand Mar didn't reply. She couldn't even tell Aunt Yenny who the groom would be. Ha!

In the silence, Aunt Yenny came to her own conclusion. She looked at me with a trace of dread in her eyes, as if I had an infectious disease. I wanted to tell her, don't worry, your sons will never catch it.

I then understood what it must have been like for your Grand Mar after the divorce, with people treating her like hazardous nuclear waste. They didn't need to say a word, they only needed to give a look they didn't even realise they were giving.

"Look at you," your Grand Mar muttered to me after we'd said goodbye. "Not even Yenny's imbecile sons would want you now."

I knew that she loved me, but I didn't think she liked me very much.

The salon never had more than three customers waiting on the plastic chairs by the window. One day, a large woman walked in, and immediately I could tell she wasn't going to fit on the little chairs, so I guided her to the spare hairdressing seat. She gave me a small smile, and I saw she was missing two teeth at the front.

Just as I was about to pick up my broom and dustpan, she turned to me. "There's a crick in my neck – do you think you could give it a bit of a rub, love?"

So I gave it a bit of a rub, in the same way I would massage your Grand Mar's back after she came home from work. Then, because your Grand Mar and Mrs Osman were still busy with other customers, I washed her hair and towel-dried it.

"What you were doing?" asked Mrs Osman when I was finished.

"Washing her hair, like you do with all customers."

"No, before that."

"I was giving her a neck massage," I replied. "She asked for one."

"What do think we are? One of those city salons? This is quick in-and-out job! Please. Don't create more slave work for us."

But a week later Mrs Garvey came back with another woman in a floral muu-muu. She pointed me out to her friend. "I heard you give special treatment here," said her friend. So I had to give her a neck massage too. But I'd got a new customer into the shop. After that, Mrs Osman wanted me to give customers waiting for their haircuts free head and shoulder massages. It made them more willing to wait. "But just the women, okay?" she said. "Not the men. We don't want them to get the wrong idea."

"What will I do when you leave to have your baby?" she moaned a week later. "Who will give the massages?"

Who indeed, I wondered, looking at Mrs Osman's long, electric-red nails, each one as well maintained as a racing car.

"Imagine," I suggested, "if we gave people instant coffee and biscuits. They would stay longer. You could even sell them an extra treatment."

"Don't be stupid," railed your Grand Mar. "Waste of money. Where they eat their biscuit and drink their coffee? A ten-dollar haircut not worth so much trouble."

"But you could get the biscuits on sale," I persisted. "Or ones that are on the supermarket specials trolley, with red stickers."

"Those are past use-by day! You want to kill customers?"
I knew your Grand Mar was just saying this to save face in front
of Mrs Osman, because she had no qualms about shopping at the
Not Quite Right store, where everything was past its expiry date.

"Nothing wrong with out-date biscuits," said Mrs Osman.
"They all filled with preservative anyway."

A few days later, I noticed a packet of biscuits by Mrs
Osman's sink. I opened it and approached the customers who
were waiting.

"Would you like a Tic Toc?"

"No, I'm trying to cut down sweets," said a Vietnamese woman.

"Would you like a Tic Toc?" I asked an older lady in a paisley dress.

"Oh, thank you, love," she said in surprise. "Haven't had one
of these in years." She told me how her kids used to love them.
"They learned to count with them."

The older women, mumsy-looking ones – Italian, Bosnian,
Tongan – were more likely than not to accept a biscuit, surprised
in their weariness by this small act of generosity.

"What is this, a blood bank?" asked Mrs Osman, but not
angrily. She gave me two dollars. "Go get more biscuits. But not
the chocolate ones."

"That girl has head for business!" she proudly declared when
I returned.

Your Grand Mar only sighed.

"So hard-working, very smart," Mrs Osman went on.
"Beautiful. Still very young too."

"Doesn't matter," said your Grand Mar, "she already been
used. Tricked! Stupid, like her own mother."

But Mrs Osman was right. I did have a head for business. Since I was never given any pocket money, when I was eight I had asked your Grand Par if I could be his assistant. "But you already are," he said.

"No, a proper one," I insisted. "One that you pay."

He chuckled. "You're too clever, Tool Kitty." He gave me two dollars for a day's work. I could make ten dollars a week during school holidays. I had thirty-four bucks by the end of the summer, a fortune to me.

But then I made the mistake of asking your Grand Mar if she would put my money in the bank for me. I made the mistake of showing off, of rubbing it in that your Grand Par had treated me like someone smart and responsible.

"Remember to open an account for me at the Commonwealth, okay?" I told her the next time she was about to go grocery shopping, handing her my small green Rainbow Brite pouch.

"Stop nagging me!" she snapped, shoving my money in her jacket pocket before she shut the door.

When she returned, she was puffing. "Help me, these bags are heavy." She had caught the bus because your Grand Par was working that day and she didn't want to interrupt him if he was earning money for us. As we were unpacking the groceries, I noticed that she had bought Burger Rings and Rice Bubbles. Maybe she was rewarding me for being so hard-working.

"Did you open my bank account? Do I have a bank book yet?" I asked.

It was as if she didn't hear me. "These tins of canned corn were on special. Looks like you'll be having your favourite soup tonight! Here, put this cheesecake in the freezer too before it melts. Fancy, eh?"

"But what about my bank book?"

"What about your bank book?"

"Where is it?"

"What do you think I used for all this food? Monopoly money?"

I cried and cried and cried that afternoon. She told me I was being a silly whinger and reminded me how much money *she* had spent on *me*, how if she tallied it all up it would pay for a million grocery shops, and how I was too selfish to want my family to eat.

When your Grand Par found out, he was really pissed off. He gave me fifty bucks and took me to the bank to get my own account. But somehow this didn't feel the same, especially when the teller-lady gave me a babyish yellow account book and bright orange Dollarmites money box. A few years later, your Grand Mar made me withdraw it all to pay for my high school uniform.

One evening, after your Grand Mar and I had finished dinner, and just before she was getting ready for her shift at Siamese Please, I made the same mistake of asking about my money. You'd think I would've learned.

"So, does Mrs Osman even pay me?"

"What do you mean? Of course she pays you."

"I've been working for four weeks and she hasn't given me a cent."

"That's because she gives it to me, in my pay."

"Well, can I have some of it?"

"What?"

"The money I earned."

"What do you want it for, huh?"

"It's my money."

"Doesn't look like you will be going to discos any time soon, girl."

"I want to buy food with it."

"What, so now I don't feed you enough?"

"I want to buy what *I* want to eat," I said.

"What you want to eat!" she scoffed. "All you want to eat are sweets and chips. We know what happened when you had that craving last time, don't we?"

"Yeah," I snapped back, "and do you know why it happened? Because you wouldn't give me any money."

"Oh! So now you're accusing me of making you into a thief?" she yelled. "You think it's my fault you steal? When I provide everything you need?"

I didn't reply.

"I'm not going to see you waste your money and your health. We'll need all we can get when the baby comes. Twenty-five dollars a week – what is that going to get you for the endless needs of a baby?"

"Then I'm not going back to work," I declared. "Not gonna be anyone's slave labourer."

"You can't quit," she said. "I helped you get free training, so that after the baby comes you can have a future for yourself and not be one of those dumbarses who live off the dole and drink all the time."

"Some training! All I do is sweep hair and massage customers."

The way I was going, I was either going to end up a street cleaner or a street walker, but I didn't say that. I didn't want to give her any more ammunition.

"You can get the skills to start your own business one day."

Yeah, she had started *her* own business, and look what happened with that. As if your Grand Mar could read my mind, she said, "White Ghosts don't care about superstitions! They don't care if you are married, divorced or knocked up. Things are going to be better for you."

All she could imagine – the pinnacle of my achievements – was me working in Mrs Osman's salon because I knew how to lure customers with cheap cookies, cookies I never even got to eat.

"I don't want to do the shit you do," I told her, wanting to inflict maximum pain. "I don't want your crappy life. You never think I'm made for anything better."

Because she didn't reply, I added, "I'm not going back tomorrow."

"We'll see about that." Your Grand Mar took her handbag, keys and an umbrella and headed out of the flat, locking it from the outside.

The next morning, while I was lying on the couch reading a *Reader's Digest* about a man who survived a bear attack, I heard your Grand Mar's key turning in the lock. She was back from Mrs Osman's early.

Crap, I thought. Any more time spent with her and I will go completely crazy. She won't even let me go to the doctor by myself.

Standing behind her was your Grand Par.

"Hey, my little Tool Kitty," he said.

I hadn't seen him in almost a year.

I dropped the magazine and burst into tears.

"You see, she's too big to walk to the bus stop now," said your Grand Mar accusingly.

Turned out, he'd come to take me to my appointment. In silence we walked down the stairs to the bottom of the flats, where he led me to a maroon Mercedes.

"I got some new wheels. Do you like it? Got it for a bargain, fixed it up myself." Unlike Ray's new car, your Grand Par's was like Dr Frankenstein's creation, cannibalised from three separate vehicles. Whereas Ray's car was the colour of liquid mercury, your Grand Par's was dried blood. Yet I bet no policeman would ever pull him over for suspected vehicle theft.

In the car, he stared straight ahead, without looking at me.

"So, how'd it happen?" he asked. "Whose is it? You wanna tell your old pa?"

I shrugged. "It doesn't matter. Too late now. He's not around."

Your Grand Par started saying all the right indignant things that a father should, but he sounded like a television dad, a bad actor reciting exaggerated lines he didn't have the conviction to finish. He'd never find Ray, and if he did, he'd never bash his face in. He'd probably just push him in a half-arsed way. I couldn't take him seriously.

"So, how's school?"

"I don't go anymore. Didn't Mum tell you?"

"So what are you doing with yerself?"

"Mum makes me work at the salon."

"What salon?"

I realised your Grand Mar hadn't told your Grand Par anything about her life, or mine.

"She works for a lady named Mrs Osman."

"I thought she was working at the Chinese restaurant."

"Yeah, that Thai place, at night. During the day, she works at the hairdressing salon. She makes me work there too, except I don't get paid."

"What the hell? You should be in school! You're a smart girl. I'm not having my daughter waste her time sweeping hair and doing shit slave work."

How did he know I swept hair? Did he want me to be beneath a bonnet, fixing cars? I knew your Grand Par wouldn't do anything about his indignation. He wasn't going to force me to go back to school, or talk to the principal at Christ Our Saviour about re-enrolling me. I knew exactly what your Grand Mar and Mrs Osman would have said about how unreliable men were, how selfish. But I had learned that no adults, even kindly ones like Mrs Stubinger, would go out of their way to help me. Their gestures were just to make themselves feel better about the job they did, or about themselves. No one wanted to get involved or come between me and your Grand Mar. I was *her* project, her responsibility.

We arrived at the clinic and he found a parking spot. "You don't need me to come in, do ya?"

"No."

"Good-o. I'll just wait in the car then."

"Okay." In some ways it was a relief, not having him there during my appointment. But if he had been the sort of father who insisted on coming in and waiting at reception, I would not have been embarrassed. I would have felt safe and protected.

He turned on the car radio before I'd even got out of the passenger seat.

Dr Masano told me the baby's movements were good and its heartbeat was strong. She let me listen on the fetoscope. *Bom bom bom bom bom bom.*

"Have you felt your baby move yet?" she asked.

"I think so." Over the past few weeks I'd sometimes had a strange sensation, like my tummy was popping corn.

"That's exactly what those early movements feel like," Dr Masano exclaimed when I told her.

"There's also blood in my poo," I confessed.

"Oh, that's normal," Dr Masano told me. "You probably have piles." They were like grapes or marbles made of skin, she explained. I imagined a disgusting bacterial vineyard in there, all throbbing veins and orbs. I almost vomited at the image.

She told me to drink plenty of water and not push too hard on the toilet. "Any other questions?"

How the hell was the baby supposed to come out of such a small hole, I wanted to ask, but didn't. I was too scared of the answer she might give.

"How'd it go?" your Grand Par asked me when I got back in the car. "No Down's syndrome or anything?"

"What?"

"I saw on the news that they can test for that kind of thing now." He looked at me. "Hmm, though it might be harder to spot on your baby, you know, because it might be born looking like you did."

"What?"

"Like, you can't tell whether it's Down's syndrome or just Asian eyes, you know what I mean?"

"No." If your Grand Par was so worried, he should have gone in with me.

"Anyway, I was waiting around this fifteen-minute park when I saw some coppers lurking about, so I thought I should move the car. Went to Macca's and got you this. Here." He handed me a McDonald's chocolate sundae.

"Thanks, Dad," I said, ripping off the lid.

"Whoa, take it easy! Slow down, Tool Kitty."

I didn't tell him that your Grand Mar wouldn't allow me to eat ice-cream because she thought the coldness would give you convulsions.

We'd arrived back at our block of flats by the time I licked the plastic cup clean. Your Grand Par turned off the engine.

"Here." He fished something out of his pocket and handed it to me. Three rolled-up green banknotes.

"Dad, I can't take this." Three hundred bucks. Over a week's wages.

"Of course you can."

"It's too much."

"It's yours. Buy yerself something nice. You have to hide it from the she-devil, though." He winked at me.

I clenched the money in my fist, willing my eyes to stop misting over, my breathing to settle. A rolling lump moved itself up my throat, like a mossy rock. I swallowed but it was no use, and my hands were too slow in unbuckling my seatbelt and opening the door.

The cheesy stench of sick filled the car, as tears puddled in my eyes.

"It's alright, it's alright," he kept telling me, patting my back. "Lucky I put down floor mats just the other day, eh?"

I wiped at my eyes with my sleeve. "I'll go upstairs and get a sponge."

"Nah, love, don't worry about it." Your Grand Par pulled a handful of McDonald's serviettes from the glovebox.

"I've wrecked your car."

"Nah, she'll be right." But his smile, I saw, was more of a grimace. "Listen, Tool Kitty, I've gotta go." Your Grand Par started up the engine. "If you could do me a favour and just wind down the window on your side, it's all good."

Upstairs, I hid my banknotes between the pages of *Walt Whitman*, where I knew your Grand Mar would never find them.

Chapter 10

My dawtah, she too big now," your Grand Mar told Mrs Osman the next day. "She can't work at the front. Wash hair, she can fall. Sweep floor, she can slip. And your customers, they see her from the window and it not look good."

"But the customers love her!"

"Maybe she can be in waxing room. She can learn new skill."

Outrage! I didn't want to be exiled to the back, where it was windowless and dark, stirring Mrs Osman's rank toffee, a bumbling worker bee making honey for the two queens out front.

"I'm just protecting you from all the dangerous chemicals," your Grand Mar hissed in our language. "Do you want the baby to be brain-damaged?"

"You don't care about whether there are chemicals or not, otherwise I wouldn't be working here," I spat back. "You're just embarrassed, and worried that one of your friends might come in and see me."

"Damn right I'm ashamed!" she said. "You are a disgrace. Why do you think Mrs Osman makes you wear the black apron? You dress like a dirty old man, and your expression could kill a horse."

"I'm not spending my days yanking hair off women's legs and backs. That's gross. Why can't they just use a razor?"

"You're not going to be doing any waxing," your Grand Mar determined. "I don't want your eyeballs filled to the brim with other people's disgusting hairy parts – the baby will end up as furry as a monkey. I'll do the waxing, and we'll just tell Mrs Osman that you're learning."

"Yeah, a really, really slow learner."

Your Grand Mar warned me that if I kept on with the ugly attitude, my baby would be born with birthmarks.

By now, the popcorn feeling inside my tummy had disappeared, and I felt like I had a goldfish swimming around in there.

Because the waxing "room" was only separated from the salon by a thin pink curtain, I could still hear your Grand Mar and Mrs Osman talking, every word.

"She lucky to have her mother here when baby comes," your Grand Mar told Mrs Osman. "I have no help when I have her. Her father's mother – useless! I have to look after her as well as Karuna."

"How sad," sighed Mrs Osman.

"And I lost most my teeth."

"How? Your husband hit you?"

"No, no. When I was pregnant I didn't drink much cow's milk, that's all." She hadn't yet got used to the taste. After I arrived, each one of her teeth started to wobble. A few weeks later, she could twist them like screws, and they popped out one by one in her hand. I had leached all her calcium, and probably made her the brittle person she was now.

*

"Look what I have for you!"

Your Grand Mar proudly handed me a warm egg, larger than a chicken's.

"What kind of egg is this, Mah?" I asked, peeling the top of the shell off.

"Balut. Good for helping the baby grow."

When I plunged my spoon in, something wet and warm and non-yolky leaked onto my finger. Jabbing the spoon in deeper, I gazed down and thought the egg was all grey and rotten. I leaned closer, then immediately dropped the terrible thing, wishing I'd never looked.

"Why did you do that?" yelled your Grand Mar. "Do you know how much that cost me?"

I'd seen a yellow lump covered with black and red veins, half a smished sac of skin and tender beak and claw, one undeveloped dead dot of an eye.

"Mah, it's got a bird in it!" I cried.

"Yes, that's a baby duck. Full of nutrients and all the good stuff."

"Sick!"

"You've got to eat it to help the baby develop."

"No way I'm eating that."

"I specially went to the Filipino supermarket to find this for you."

"I'm going to chuck up. It's animal cruelty. It's an abortion duck egg!"

In the end, your Grand Mar ate the balut. She just popped the whole mass of feather and claw into her mouth and chewed it a few times and swallowed. I gagged just watching her.

"Stop carrying on like that," she said to me.

She also ate the yolk, but gave me the solidified egg white at the base. That was the one thing I would agree to eat. It had the consistency of a rubbery chicken joint and didn't taste like much.

Your Grand Mar sighed. "You missed out on the best part."

Some girls came into Caramel salon expecting a haircut to change them in unimaginable ways, and walked out with three centimetres lopped off. They kept touching their hair as if they were half-bald. Others who got buzz cuts or dyed their hair bright green walked out like they were the same as before, no big deal.

Your Grand Mar had been telling me for weeks that my hair was getting too long, so I thought it was just another of her whinges about me looking unkempt. Besides, my hair had never looked healthier – it was so racehorse thick and shiny that Mrs Osman's overhead lights reflected off it.

"The longer your hair is, the more nutrients it is sapping from the baby," your Grand Mar told me.

"That's completely nuts, Mah."

"It's true! Your body takes energy away from building the baby and uses it for growing hair. It's time for you to get a haircut. Who do you need to grow your hair for now, huh?"

"It's my hair. Leave it alone."

But she was serious, and made me sit on a chair at the salon when there were no customers. When your Grand Mar was done, I had a Chinese Communist Party bob, with a fringe so short that it looked like I'd escaped from Sunbury Asylum.

Even Mrs Osman could not offer one of her flippant, honeyed compliments. All she said was, "Don't worry, darling, it will grow back."

That's when I decided I would take your Grand Par's money and run away. I knew there were homes for expectant teenage mothers. I'd read about them in a book. To be honest, the one I'd read about sounded terrible – the girls were locked up by nuns, fed gruel and made to do laundry. There was no way I was going to one of those places. The safest place for me would be with your Grand Par. After all, there must be a reason he'd given me all that money. Knowing what your Grand Mar would say and do, he was probably just too embarrassed to ask me to stay with him. But if I made my way to him, proving that I was resourceful and dedicated, he would not send me back. He would not lock me in his house, or care what I wore or ate or did. He'd just spend all day working on his cars, and then take me to Hungry Jack's for dinner. We would have a peaceful, wordless existence.

But that evening, when I got home, the money your Grand Par had given me was gone. It wasn't in the Whitman, beneath our mattress or between the cupboard and the wall.

I panicked. Maybe we had been robbed. But the door was secure; no one had broken in.

"I knew you had been hiding something from me," your Grand Mar said. She was standing by the doorway.

I turned to face her. "You stole my money!"

"How selfish. To have so much money and to keep it all

hidden when I work like a slave just to support you. Everything I do is for you."

"That money is mine," I said. "Dad gave it to me!"

"Yes? And what were you going to do with it, huh? What will you spend it on?"

"Give it back!"

"I can't. Most of it's gone on the rent, water and electricity. Do you think it's cheap to stay alive, have clean clothes, keep warm? And what about after you have the baby? Where are we going to get money for the herbs and pigs' feet to make soup for you?"

When you are born, I can probably get my own money from the government, I thought. In my own bank account.

"I don't know why you keep this rotting old book," your Grand Mar told me, "but I'm not stupid. I know you don't read it, that you go to the library every week to get new books. So I thought, why would she keep a dirty old book she doesn't even look at, that she probably picked up from a kerbside dump? There must be another reason. And sure enough, when I shook the book, what should come fluttering out but all this money. A week's wages!"

"It was mine!"

"Fine. Tell your father," she challenged me. "Go on. Ask him to give you some more. It's about time he paid some support. Then I won't have to work to death. See how much money you can get from him while I work myself to death for you."

"I never asked you to!"

"If he loves you so much," said your Grand Mar, "why don't you ask him to let you live with him? See what he says!"

"I will!"

*

"I think we'll be adventurous and catch public transport today, Tool Kitty."

Your Grand Par had arrived to take me to my regular check-up with Dr Masano, and he was talking to me like I was seven. I knew he didn't want another accident in his car.

On the bus, the furry-faced, slurry-voiced man in front of us turned around, resting his arm on the back of his seat, and stared. "Mate, how much didya pay fer your wife?"

His breath smelled like my locker the time I accidentally left some chicken soup in it over the term break.

"What?" said your Grand Par.

"How much didya buy ya wife fer?"

Your Grand Par glared at him.

"She's sweet as."

"She's my daughter, you sick fuck!"

He winked at your Grand Par and looked meaningfully at my belly. Your Grand Par was about to get up and clobber him one, but the guy held up his hands in defence.

"Aww, mate, I was jes kidding. I'm sorry I pissed you off. She's a real knockout, your daughter. Your missus must be hot as. You lucky bastard."

A half-smile switched on your Grand Par's face, like he couldn't help himself.

"Stupid drunk arsehole," muttered your Grand Par when we stepped off the bus, but I could tell by the brisk way he was walking, not even waiting for me to catch up, that he was embarrassed to have a knocked-up teenage daughter.

He almost tripped across a rolled-up shape on the ground. A cardboard sign rested on the middle of the sleeping mass:

Hi my name is Tess I am 12 weeks pregnant and homeless.

So this was what happened when you ran away and had nowhere to go. I wished I had something to give her. I remembered those early days, the smells. I could enter a public toilet and immediately know whether the last person in each cubicle had done a number one or two.

"She's just lying," muttered your Grand Par. "Look at her, sleeping so close to a hospital. She could easily go in and get some help there. She doesn't even look pregnant, she looks like a druggie."

"One and a half months to go, Karuna," Dr Masano told me. "Are you still looking after yourself?"

"Yes."

"Eating properly?"

"Yes."

Your Grand Mar had started cooking more and more vegetables, and pork and fish. She no longer let me eat the take-away from Siamese Please. "All that MSG will damage the baby's brain," she said. "All those black beans will make her dark."

"Still working at the hairdresser?" asked Dr Masano.

"Yes, but my mum will make me take the last month off. She says I need to rest."

"That's good," said Dr Masano. "You do need to take it easy in the last month."

"But I'm going to be so bored stuck in the flat all day, every day."

"Oh honey, it's not that long, even though it might seem

like it now. Besides, you could always go for walks in the neighbourhood. It's good to get in some exercise. Believe me, the fitter you are, the better prepared you'll be for pushing out that baby."

Dr Masano put the stethoscope on my belly. Where once you sounded like wild horses galloping, now you sounded like a ticking bomb. *Kaboom, kaboom, kaboom.*

Your Grand Par took me to McDonald's for lunch afterwards as a treat.

"Go easy there!" he said. "You don't want it to come back out again like last time, eh?"

I kept shoving fries in my mouth, three at a time.

"Your mum not feeding you enough?"

Your Grand Mar fed me fine, just not the sort of food pregnant teenagers craved.

"Is she feeding you that weird fruit that looks like a Viking mallet? The one that's like sitting on the toilet eating custard?"

I'd never thought of durian that way before. I couldn't stand the stuff, and now I knew why. I couldn't help smiling.

"Had it once," said your Grand Par. "Never again. But geez, that shit's expensive." He laughed at his own joke.

I tried to tell him about how nuts your Grand Mar had become.

"Aw, she's always been nuts," said your Grand Par. "Does she smack you?"

"No. But she tries to control everything!"

"That's just the way she is."

"Yeah, but you could leave her and I can't. She won't let me do normal stuff. The other day she wouldn't even let me watch *Alvin and the Chipmunks*. 'Do you want the baby to be deformed?' she said. 'Do you want it to come out looking like those terrible animals? Turn it off now.'"

Your Grand Par chuckled. "Ha! Her hocus-pocus backwater ways. I remember those all too well. Whenever I got sick, she told me to drink coconut water coz my blood was too hot or something. If you got a blood nose, she'd say I'd fed you too much chocolate. When she was pregnant with you, she wouldn't drink Coke because she said she didn't want you to turn out black. Batshit crazy woman."

"What's your phone number, Dad?"

There was a slight pause. "Your mum has it already, love."

So it wasn't just your Grand Mar he wanted to leave him alone – it was me too. He thought I was an endless pit of need like your Grand Mar. He knew that your Grand Mar wouldn't pass on his number, would not want me to contact him.

"Don't worry, I'm not going to ask you for money," I muttered bitterly.

He pretended to be shocked. Taking out the biro from his pocket, he scrawled some digits on a McDonald's serviette. "Here it is," he told me, "keep it in case. But mind you, I won't be using it for long."

"How come?"

"I'm moving up to Wodonga," he said.

"But why?" I thought that because he was spending more time with me, he was back in my life, that he'd be back for the birth of his grandchild, and eventually we'd become close again, close enough for him to offer me a haven in his home. It wasn't fair!

"Change of scenery, I guess."

"Can I stay with you for a while, Dad? Before you move?"

"Wha—?"

"Mum's crazy. She's threatened to lock me up next month."

"Karuna," he said, stern like a teacher. Car Ruiner. Wrecker of his mobility, the one who eternally chained him to your Grand Mar. But now I was no longer a child; he didn't have to care about me anymore. I would not get hit by traffic dashing across the road, did not need money for school supplies. And my child was my responsibility. "You know I'd have you stay with me if I could. But my place is no place for a teenage girl having a baby. And I'm moving really soon, in about three months' time."

I wasn't going to cry, but I wasn't going to tell him I understood either. It was not my job to make my father feel better for not giving a crap about me.

"Would you like a strawberry milkshake?" he asked.

"I don't drink those anymore, Dad," I said. I hadn't had one since I was ten and realised they tasted nothing like strawberries and more like the colour pink.

"For old time's sake then," he coaxed.

"No, thanks."

"Well, I'll get you a couple more burgers to take away. Hide them from the she-devil, though, she'll tell you that you don't need them."

How the hell was I going to hide two Big Macs from your Grand Mar around our flat? But I let him buy them for me. I realised what I was doing – I was going to milk your Grand

Par for all I could, and in this way I guessed I was no different from your Grand Mar.

"See you later, Karuna," he said to me when we arrived back at our flats.

I took my warm paper bag of hamburgers and left his car without looking back.

Chapter 11

One day two girls I recognised from Christ Our Saviour, Jana and Connie, came in to get their hair done for their school formal. I was glad to be out the back, unpacking an industrial box of shampoo bottles and stacking them on the shelf beneath the bulk toilet paper. This Cinderella didn't even know there was a ball.

But after I'd packed away the supplies, I went into the empty waxing room, and through an opening in the curtain I could see Connie, hair hot and crispy around her face like the Chow Mein from Siamese Please. "Will said he's gonna wear a corsage to match my dress," she was telling Jana.

The girls, they looked so young and beautiful. Funny how when I was at school, besides the clear-cut obvious beauties, all I could see of other girls was when they had a bad spell of pimples, or if their teeth were whiter than mine, or if their hair had a nice curl to it. Things I coveted and things I detested in myself, like I was looking at them through a microscope, zooming in on different parts. Now I saw them for what they were – young, free, uncomplicated, yet through my new telescopic lens, they also seemed so distant.

"You want a blow job?" your Grand Mar asked, waving her hair dryer.

"What?"

"A blow job?"

Connie looked at Jana and smirked. Stupid dumb bitch, pretending not to understand.

"For free," your Grand Mar added.

The smirk turned into a gummy red slice-of-watermelon smile. I could already imagine the story Connie would tell her table at the formal – *I went to this Asian hairdresser and you'll never believe what she offered me . . .*

I went back inside the storeroom and shut the door, the whirr of the hair dryer still coming through like an angry fly.

"She said her dress cost two hundred and forty dollars," said Mrs Osman, after the girls had left. "Can you believe those Aussies?" I could hear them through the door – when there were no customers Mrs Osman and your Grand Mar's conversations were like the TV turned up full volume.

"Huh, those Ghosts," your Grand Mar scoffed. "This is why they are so poor." But those girls, I knew, weren't poor at all. Their parents owned modest furniture stores or worked as accountants. "Small by small we save up, and we can get a house, move out of crappy flat."

I poked my head around the door. "Little by little, you mean," I said, but they had no idea what I was talking about.

Mrs Osman walked up to me and put both her hands on my shoulders. "Come here. You sad, I know you are." She made an exaggerated pouting face. "See those girls all dress beautiful for their school dance. Let me help you. Come, come. Sit. Sit down." She marched me by my shoulders into the salon and pushed me onto a vinyl chair. "You still very beautiful, even more beautiful than they. Maybe time for some make-up for you, pretty angel."

Your Grand Mar spoke up roughly. "No. No need."

"What you mean, no need? She work so hard, she deserve some fun."

Make-up, of course, had never been fun for your Grand Mar. It had been her livelihood and her craft, and later, one of the biggest losses in her life.

"She don't need no more. Who's going to see, huh?"

It was then that I knew for sure what I had suspected all along. My looks were the only thing of worth to your Grand Mar, but now that they were valueless currency she no longer cared. She had given up on me. It was like putting icing sugar on an inedible cake. She wouldn't even look at me.

But Mrs Osman was kind. She said, "You stupid woman, who can stop staring at a face like this one? Her big belly is not forever." She opened up her black make-up case and uncapped a jar of foundation. The sponge brushed my face in little circles, like a magic wand.

"Those Aussies, they good at spending," noted Mrs Osman, "but big spender should also be big earner."

I blocked my ears from their philosophising, and thought about Ray in his Thriller jacket, his tight smile and twinkling eyes. But even this no longer held me in its thrall. It was like conjuring up the image of a pop singer, someone I'd never meet in real life.

"You my apprentice," said Mrs Osman. "Learn carefully." She loaded up a brush with a deep rose blush and began sweeping from just in front of my ears to the middle of my cheek. "To bring out cheekbones," she said.

Your Grand Mar watched without saying a word. She knew she was better. She would not have used just one tone, but blended in three, and dusted the sides of my nose with a slightly deeper bronze as well. Mrs Osman worked on my eyebrows with a brown pencil. She ran a black eyeliner across the inner rim of my lower eyelid.

"You a good model," she said. She mascaraed my eyes and lined my lips, then filled them in a deep fuchsia. Holding a mirror up to my face, she said, "Wah, now you look like a Persian princess!"

No one besides your Grand Mar had ever made up my face.

"I take picture," said Mrs Osman. "She can be on our window."

"I don't want her face to be on no window."

"That face will help us get customer!" said Mrs Osman.

"My dawtah not be on any window. No, please. Thank you."

With my made-up face, fat belly and god-awful haircut, I felt like a joke without a punchline, something no one would even laugh at because I was so pathetic. An egg on legs.

"Oh, don't cry," said Mrs Osman, "tears will make mascara river down your face!"

"Don't worry," said your Grand Mar, "you not see this misery face long anyway. She going to rest at home for the last month."

I'd spent most of the last three years trying to get away from your Grand Mar, and now I was with her all the time. We slept in the same bed, we woke up together, we went to work together, we came home and ate together, and then we slept in the same bed again. She watched my every move like a deranged film director forced into directing a movie she knew would be a flop. I knew that for the next month it would just be me and you and her, coexisting with the only other living things in this flat, the mould and the bacteria. I was just the incubator. After you came out, there'd be no need for me anymore – your Grand Mar would take over completely. You would be the fresher, better version of me, a new model straight out of its packaging. I would be the shredded cardboard box, the type we used to line our cupboards – there to absorb spills and stains, but mostly hidden from view.

On my last day of work, I could no longer see my own two feet beneath my black apron. By now the goldfish inside me seemed to have transformed into a big fat lumbering carp, and I didn't like when it nudged my ribs.

When your Grand Mar was having her two-minute noodles for lunch in the back room and there were no customers out the front, Mrs Osman sat me down in the vinyl chair again.

"Must be tiring for you standing up now," she said gently, stroking my hair.

I wanted to purr like a cat; I hadn't been touched for so long.

She sighed. "I'm going to miss you, sweet Karuna. Even before we meet, I feel like I know you because your mother talk about you all the time. Actually when she first come in for the job, she bring her photo books to show me. One book was all pictures of you."

I burned with embarrassment. That damned book.

"Ha, your mother. She got the job because of that book. She had a crazy look in her eyes, like she was just going to stay in my salon until I give her work. I know she will not nick off on me after few months like those useless nineteen-year-olds I have before. And then she say she want to bring her daughter to work. First I tell her no. I think she is trying to get more money from me, to bring in her little princess with darling soft hands. But then you turn up, and you are nothing like I expect. So hard-working! So clever!"

For the first time I realised I might miss Mrs Osman, the only other constant adult in my life these last few months.

"You need to make sure you feel your baby kick every day," Mrs Osman told me. "And call doctor if you don't."

I didn't mind when Mrs Osman gave me advice; she didn't do it like your Grand Mar.

"If I had daughter," she sighed, "she would be your age." She patted my shoulders. "You are very special girl, Karuna. Beautiful, healthy, smart, with a new baby soon. Your mother is very lucky to have you."

I wished Mrs Osman had not said that. It dislodged a plug I'd deliberately shoved into my heart in order to stop the deluge of frightening thoughts about my future – our future.

"Mrs Osman," I said quietly, "my mother says when my baby's born, she's going to make my baby believe that I'm the sister."

"I know, she tell me this all the time. She says is best for you. You still too young. You have good life ahead of you."

"But I won't. I won't have anything left of my own!"

"Don't say that, sweet."

"It's true. She wants to control everything!"

"Listen, Karuna." Mrs Osman turned my chair around and looked me in the eye. "Your baby will still be your baby. It will say so on the birth certificate. Is this true or not?"

"Yes."

"So when that baby grow to be adult, he can read for himself the truth. True or not?"

"Yes." Why hadn't I thought of something so obvious?

"Unless you lock him at home like a dumb thing. Will you do that?"

"No!"

"Of course not. And you must get yourself smarter, go back to school. The more a mother know, the smarter her kid will be. And at school, you don't want boys to think you an easy girl. They will if they know you already have a baby. You also don't want your baby growing up around a hair salon, do you, stuck with you and two bossy old perm-hair grannies? There, ha! So nice to see you smile again! Listen, I have something small-small for you."

I thought that the bounty she dropped in my lap would be sample shampoos and conditioners. But inside the unassuming brown paper bag were Tim Tams, blocks of Cadbury, Ferrero Rochers and Arnott's biscuits.

"Woah, the motherlode," I whispered.

"Oh, just snacks," she said. "You need to dig deeper." She reached inside the bag and pulled out a lavender hardcover notebook with gold lettering on the cover: *L'Oréal: Because I'm Worth It.* "For you to use when you go back to school next year," she explained. "Free gift when I buy hair dye. Nice, eh?"

Next emerged a glass pendant of concentric blue circles, attached to a silver chain. "This is the evil eye charm. It keep away bad looks, people who want to take your happy away. For protect you and the baby."

"Thanks, Mrs Osman."

I held onto it, knowing that in my isolation next month it would only be directing its glare at one other person.

As if she could read my terrible thoughts, Mrs Osman suddenly said, "You know, Karuna. Your mother may not know how to love you the best. But she love you the most."

Now

Chapter 12

It's the sweeping-tail end of winter and your Grand Mar has locked me in the flat. She says she is doing this to protect me, and I should be more grateful. It's cold outside, says your Grand Mar, I could freeze the baby to death. She still can't trust me to be out and about, who knows what authorities I'd dob her in to next, after the fiasco at Christ Our Saviour College. She tells me it's my own damn fault, that I made this bed, now I should lie in it. But there is no need for me to lie in any bed. Dr Masano even said so. Dr Masano told me that I should stay on my feet, walk around, do squats. She says that my muscles down there need to be trained for the marathon of labour.

"Squatting is what druggies do on park benches," your Grand Mar tells me when she finds out. "Don't listen to her."

But Dr Masano is the only adult I trust now that Mrs Osman is gone.

There is not much for me to do now but remember stuff from my past. "Re-member-ing" sounds like putting arms and legs back together. It makes me think of that bad egg Humpty Dumpty, how no one could make him whole again after he shattered. I know I have to break open for you to come out, but I don't want to think about that.

Every evening, your Grand Mar returns from the salon at around six to bring me dinner, then gets changed and goes out to work at Siamese Please. At half-past midnight or one she returns, and I am still awake. When she calls out my name, I feel something cold and hard shoot up my spine.

"Just practising my writing," I say, when your Grand Mar takes Mrs Osman's lavender notebook from me and flicks through the pages.

"It's getting worse, not better," she says to me, jabbing a finger at my last entry. The words tumble down the lines like someone has taken a hammer to a shelf and its contents. "You're not trying hard enough anymore." I know that my thoughts are falling off the edge, but I have no idea how to fix the shelf.

"You shouldn't have sharp objects like pens in the bed," she scolds. "The baby might be born with a cleft lip. Also, you shouldn't be awake at this hour."

I can't get to sleep at night because I do nothing all day and nothing ever happens. With all these hours to kill instead of live, what can I do except write in here? I'm not even sure whether I do this for you or me. Once I've got everything down, I worry that I'll be completely emptied of thoughts. Will nothing happen to me except this endless waiting?

I have about a month to go and then your Grand Mar says she will lock me up for another two months when you come. One hundred days. It's no time at all, she tells me, but she's not the one waiting, she can't even catch a falling minute. She's always working, and anyway time goes by so much faster the older you get. "I'm so busy," your Grand Mar is always railing, "so busy all the time that it feels like I'm rush-rushing towards

death. When you have children, you'll understand these things."
I know that one year for a two-year-old is half of their life, but
a year to a sixty-year-old is only one sixtieth of their life, and so
three months to a sixteen-year-old . . . I'm too tired to work this
stuff out.

Every time I blink, my eyelids make a clicking sound like
turning off a light switch behind a closed door. I'm sure I need
eye drops or something, but I have no energy to ask. At night,
I feel like that princess on top of the seventeen mattresses, toss-
ing and turning, except the pea is inside me and I can definitely
feel it.

"I'm working so hard now," your Grand Mar tells me, "so
that after you give birth, I can take the month off and look after
you. You have no idea how lucky you are. My own mother wasn't
there for me when I had you." Both her parents were dead by
then. I wonder if she wishes they could have met me. I wonder
whether they were as mean as she is.

This flat has the pissy smell of damp clothes that have not
been aired properly. I wish it was like the inside of a Kmart
store: every corner lit up, every object in its rightful place, no
sticky, greasy veneer. I spend my time cleaning. Washing the
dishes, I feel like a tugboat – I have to lean into the sink, over
my belly, the water splashing around us onto the floor. I feel
like a person with a buoy wrapped around me. A girl overboard.

I ask your Grand Mar if we can clean out the spare room
so that you will have a nursery, but she tells me not to be
ridiculous, that babies always sleep in the same bed as their
mums. "Whoever heard of putting them in a different room?
People with too much time, space and money," she scoffs.

"Most of the world sleep with their babies in the same bed. All animals do."

Now that she's locked me in, all I have left is the television, but even that depresses me. *Like sands through the hourglass, so are the days of our lives.* What crap is this? Adults have no frigging imagination, spending millions making shows about people in make-up standing around in darkened rooms talking about drama, with no actual drama happening. More shit happens in the commercials: Fairstar the Fun Ship – *There's so much fun on the one ship!*

One unrelenting afternoon, I'm paying little attention to the happy families singing the praises of Sorbent – Australia's softest tissue, a house with Pebblemix floors, Cadbury Roses to congratulate your mum for being your mum. The next moment, my heart stops.

How can they show something like this on television, during the day? I have to wait until the next commercial break to confirm that I haven't imagined such a nightmare. People knocked over like bowling balls, open-eyed corpses swept away, the background foggy darkness. The Grim Reaper in the centre, killing everyone – men, women, children.

Could someone as clean as Ray kill me?

I wonder whether he has seen the same ad, and what he'd be thinking. I hope it has scared the shit out of him as well. That would serve him right.

I shakily walk to the kitchen, pick up the phone, and frantically dial.

The receptionist picks up. "I need to talk to Dr Masano, please, Kathy. It's Karuna. Karuna Kelly."

"Is this an emergency, honey?"

"I think so."

"Dr Masano," I blurt when she comes on the line, "will I die of AIDS?"

"Karuna, what?"

"Do I have AIDS?"

"Did your partner have AIDS?"

"No! I don't think so."

"What makes you think you have AIDS?"

"The commercial said it can kill any of us. At any time."

"Karuna, I don't think you are HIV-positive."

"I don't want to die of AIDS." I begin to cry. "I just don't want to die."

"Karuna, it's okay. You are not going to die."

"What if I do? I don't want to die."

"You are going to get through this pregnancy fine."

"It's all so scary. I'm not sure I can do it."

"I understand. Pregnancy is a frightening time, even for grown-up women who've had many children. You are young and strong, and you can do it."

I wipe my eyes on my sleeve, feeling ridiculous for getting panicked by a stupid ad. When I hang up, I feel only a little better, but the little is enough to make me fall asleep.

"What are you doing?" your Grand Mar asks when she returns from the salon, seeing me slumped on the couch with the TV on. "If you won't turn it off, at least watch something that will make the baby smarter. Turn it to the news."

But on the news there's always bad stuff happening. An evil Knight slays seven innocents in Clifton Hill. Police raid a lakeside paradise and find a group of pale, platinum-topped storybook orphans hidden from the world. The news will not make you smarter, I think, it will just make you want to crawl back inside.

One afternoon I find a letter with the stamp not post-marked. Some marketing material from a cleaning company, which I throw away. But I cut the stamp from the envelope and soak it in a bowl of boiling water until it reluctantly un-clings from the paper like a drowned beloved, floating sadly to the top. The stamp shows two ginger-haired kids catching a yabby.

Dear Tweezer, I am going to have my baby in a month and my mum has locked me in the house.

No, no, no, because I remember that her brother or father will probably look through the mail and find out that the cursed fox is back for their lamb. Last time I saw Tweezer, how I tow-ered over her. She seemed more like a dumb little sister than my once best friend.

Dear Mr and Mrs Rodriguez, I would greatly appreciate if you could tell me how to contact your son so I can let him know I am eight months pregnant with his baby.

Raymond Rodriguez – what were his parents' first names? There are at least twenty entries for Rodriguez in the White Pages, and I only have this one stamp. I have to use it wisely, like a girl with only one wish. I open up Whitman's jacket and put the stamp between two pages.

I know that no one can really help me.

I am an upside-down question mark, like those ones Spanish people use to begin question-sentences. My dot for a head, my fat belly from the side.

I have no answers to anything.

So here we are, this notebook getting fatter and fatter just like me.

The other day your Grand Mar took out a cardboard box of all my baby clothes she'd kept, fussy things with frills and matching bonnets. Poor you, unable to complain about the discomfort of a ribbon cutting in beneath your chin, or a fake mother-of-pearl button squished between the folds in the back of your neck.

Now I think, why should your Grand Mar be allowed to do this to you? *You're not her baby. You're mine!* I begin counting down the days to when she will take you away. You are safe inside me now, but when you come out, she's going to repeat everything she did with me, but to you, and you can't fail her or else.

I really and truly hope that you'll be a boy, because your Grand Mar will have no idea what to do with such a creature. Maybe she won't bother about you – or bother you – so much. She might not care if you're grotty, or if you want to play ball sports. Like Rumpelstiltskin in reverse, she might not want to claim you for herself.

The last time I saw Dr Masano she told me that you will probably turn this month, which means that your kicking legs will be nearer to my heart, your head closer to gravity and the ground.

I had to catch a bus there by myself, and on the way back, the bus stopped at the lights for a long while. Looking out the window, I saw a birthday party underway in the park across the street. All the family and friends were sitting on picnic rugs. There must have been at least ten mats, connected like continents. I saw some actual picnic baskets too – the square, straw sort padded inside with gingham, and spoons and forks and knives held with elastic to the top of the lid.

It was a party for a baby, a fat baby in a white shirt and little corduroy overalls. They held him up to the sky, passed him around. All that love, I thought, for one tiny person. How can I compete? How can your Grand Mar? There are only the two of us, and much of the time we don't even like each other. But here we are, waiting to bomb you with our flawed, anxious, inadequate love.

I have reordered time, I have turned the world upside-down, and I have done it all for you, Jareth says to Sarah. *Just fear me, love me, do as I say and I will be your slave.* He is so adult, so large and looming and tall, and she is so young and small. I can't believe that I'd once wished the Goblin King would smile his pointy, beige-toothed smile at me and come and whisk me away. He's a sly trickster – how could an adult be enslaved by a fifteen-year-old?

But this is no Jim Henson fairytale. No ogre or evil stepmother is going to take you away from me, only your Grand Mar herself; and she'll tell you a different story about your life so you won't know any better, and by the time you're old enough to understand, you probably won't believe me.

Your Grand Mar is sometimes a massive piece of work, not a nice piece of Jesus carpentry but some stony, dark tablet created by slaves two thousand years ago, with carvings in a language no one can read but her. That's why she is called Grand Mar. Big Mistake. She exists to remind me of all the ones I have made. What point is there to having dreams of my own?

Now I can't even read more than a few sentences without feeling muddle-headed and despairing. I know all the things I am missing out on, the things an ordinary teenager gets to feel and experience. I am stuck, stuck, stuck. I feel as though I have fallen in a hole and can't get back out. People – teachers, friends, doctors – have peered at me from above the hole but their arms are not long enough to haul me up. They wave and think they are helping but all they are doing is blocking out the light.

It's no use.

Nothing helps.

I can't write anymore.

I've run out of words.

So there is nothing much for me to do but sleep like a hibernating animal, hoping I won't die in the frost, hoping I will wake up in spring, hoping to survive this nine-month midnight with no memory of how past springs look or feel or smell or taste.

Chapter 13

No wonder movies make it romantic, skip to visions of flower buds opening. You are caught in between my shit and piss holes, marinated in blood and steaming juices, warm and rank as the inside of a stranger's mouth, and you are stuck.

Fuck. Your Grand Mar, making me spend that last month locked in. Now, with my muscles all shrunk snug like a swaddle around you, you don't want to come out. The waves of pressure keep coming and it hurts so much I think I am going to die.

"Push, push!" shouts the midwife, "you can do it, Mum," and in my befuddled state I think, yeah, Mah, why aren't *you* doing it? Why aren't *you* pushing?

Because how could *I* possibly be a mum?

"I can't do it," I gasp. "I can't."

I can't even breathe properly.

Oh my God. At Christ Our Saviour, the nuns told us that Eve ate the forbidden fruit and created suffering. I feel like I've swallowed a whole orchard, stems and all, and it's suddenly come to life, trying to break through my stomach skin. The appley nubs of your nudging limbs, the grapey hernias, the durian-sharp spikes of pain.

In the end, the doctor has to slit me open to yank your head through. "Just a little cut," he says, "a small sting."

Your Grand Mar is there with me, but the moment she sees the blaze of light along the blade, her eyeballs roll upward and she sways back. Almost a cartoon swoon. A nurse catches her by the shoulders, helps her out of the room.

I expect a bellow below, but it is not even a cat's miaow. *Meh, meh, meh, meh*, you come out saying, more of a hiccup than a howl. Then they cut you free, put you high on my chest, and you move your head from side to side, as if saying *no, no, no, no* to being in the world, you'd rather go back in. Too bad, mister, that cave is closed. After I push out the grisly flayed meat-bag that is the placenta, the surgeon stitches me up.

"What a beautiful girl!" the midwife cries.

Your toothless mouth is as pink as a kitten's when you yawn. Your eyes are all dark grey iris, like an alien. Your arms and legs are still folded like a frog's and flail jerkily, as if you can't understand why my belly is no longer around you. Your skin is adhesive and clings to me like a sticker I've earned through hard work. You smell like yoghurt.

You are the most wonderful thing I have ever seen.

"Do you have a name for her?" asks the midwife.

I hadn't expected you to be a girl.

"No. Do I have to name her now?"

"Of course not, love. No need to panic. You have a few weeks to decide. It's just that most mothers already have names picked out."

How long until your Grand Mar comes in again? I do not want to hand you over to her. I do not want to do that because you are my baby, and even though I know she's going to take you anyway, I don't want to be the one to give you to her. I give you to the midwife instead, who reassures me that after you're cleaned up, she'll bring you right back in. I know this is probably the only time I'll get to spend with you alone.

"Can you tell my mother to come back later?" I ask the midwife. "I'm tired, and I know she will just fuss around me."

"Sure, honey. I know what new grandmas are like! No visitors for you for the next two hours, then."

"Thanks. But can I still have my baby with me?"

"Of course."

I can't believe what I've made. I want to see you again, straightaway, so that I know you're real. They take me to a curtained room with a clean bed, and when you are wheeled back in a little plastic tub, I pick you up. The best thing about you is your smell. I call it a micious smell because no word exists yet to describe its musty deliciousness. It's funny how they say babies are so trusting, because you look like a paranoid old man who's scared someone will pinch his life savings from beneath his mattress. But you can have your secret thoughts, I think. That way you will constantly surprise me.

I am bigger than you, the upper-case letter of our word. But you have become the exclamation point to my life.

When you close your eyes, I finally close mine and go to sleep.

When I wake up, you are not in your plastic tub. I scoot upright and sit on my pillow, feeling a sharp sting. Your Grand Mar is sitting in a green chair, holding you. She's clucking at you like you are a chick and she is the hen.

She looks up. "You're awake."

"Let me hold her, Mah." How had she gotten in?

It's as if she doesn't hear me. "Get your bum off the pillow, you'll soil it, make it bloody."

Perhaps I had expected your arrival to shift something in your Grand Mar – for her to see me as someone different, someone capable of creating such a small and perfect creature and being its mother. But now, without a doubt, I know she is exactly the same – pointing out all the ways I would do things wrong, ruin things.

A new nurse comes in, and I wonder what happened to the midwife who'd promised to keep your Grand Mar away. She is one of the very first people you have seen in your new life and I don't even know her name.

"Hey there, you're awake. I'm Margaret, and I'll be taking care of you during this shift." She sees your Grand Mar holding you. "Awww."

"Can I hold her?" I ask Nurse Margaret.

"Of course." She walks over to your Grand Mar.

"No, she has stitch," your Grand Mar protests. "She need to rest."

"It's okay, Grandma. The stitches don't affect her ability to hold her baby." Margaret shows me how, and then you are back in my arms, and I take in the small, black sequins of your eyes, and your milky cat yawn.

How large a planet I am, looming over this little soul, like an eclipse. My shadow can completely cover you if I am not careful,

I realise, leaving you cold. I vow then and there never to hover over you and block your light.

Your Grand Par comes to visit the next day, but mostly stands around with his hands in his pockets, jingling coins. Your Grand Mar leaves the room when she sees him, telling me she is going to heat up some rice in the microwave for my lunch. "Hospital only gives you party food," she mutters, looking distastefully at my jelly cup, orange juice and tub of fruit salad.

He doesn't come too close, just peers at me holding you. "She's a little beauty, hey?"

I don't think he's even taken a proper look at your face.

"Can I get you anything, love?" your Grand Par asks.

"A Mars Bar from the vending machine, please."

"Right-o."

When he returns, he puts my treat on the little tray table beside my bed.

"Don't eat it all at once, eh?"

Ha, I think. Very generous, Dad.

But after he leaves, when I hide the Mars Bar under my pillow before your Grand Mar's return, I discover he's folded a one-hundred-dollar note into a small rectangle beneath.

Your Grand Mar returns with a plastic container – she's made me ginger and pork, rice and spinach. "I'll hold the baby while you eat," she tells me. I am surprisingly ravenous.

She rubs your twiggy arm, and I catch her furrowing her brow even though she is clucking love at you. I know what she sees. You are not white, not even a mellow yellow. Your skin is like your father's, Nestlé Coffee and Milk. But she doesn't say anything.

Three nights later, I feel like a grown-up version of a Cabbage Patch Kid, one leaf on each aching boob. I'd thought that by the time you came out I'd be cow-heavy with milk for you, but it didn't happen. Just when I think you will starve, my chest feels blocked with cement. Great, I think, another way my machinery is defective.

"That's just your milk coming in," explains Nurse Margaret during her shift. "Cabbage leaves will ease the pain."

The next day you are sucking away, deflating me like a balloon.

"Nurse her every three hours," says Nurse Margaret. "Don't let her control you."

"Feed her only the bottle," says your Grand Mar. "It's best for her, cleaner. Also, formula is given for free in hospital, so make the most of it while you can."

"The nurse said that —"

"Look at your shrunken water-balloon boobs," your Grand Mar accuses. "There's nothing to fill her up on."

But the milk leaks out like hot, white tears. Your little head moves from side to side on my chest like you are saying *no, no, no,* but what you are really doing in your butting-marsupial way is looking for a feed.

"If you don't bottle-feed her, how do you expect to sleep through the night?"

"What do you mean, sleep through the night?" I ask. "Babies have to be fed every three hours, the nurse said!"

"Nonsense. You need to recover from all the lost blood. You sleep through the night and I will wake up to feed her."

I grip you tighter. "You're not feeding her."

"I'm only doing this for your own good, so you can get some rest, you stupid girl."

I know if I let go, she'll get you onto the bottle and then there'll be no need for me anymore, and I won't be able to hold you when I want to.

"She's not a toy," your Grand Mar yells. "Don't hold her so tightly, you'll suffocate her!"

You start to wail.

Of course you're not a toy. I grew up playing with neckless rubber baby dolls whose arms and legs were rigid. You're floppier than I ever imagined.

"Stop shouting so loud," I hiss. "See, you scared her."

"At least put her down so she can sleep properly."

When your Grand Mar takes you from my arms, you immediately stop crying. I resent her even more. I watch her put you back inside your plastic tub.

"For goodness sake, don't start crying now if you know what's good for you. Childbirth weakens the liver, which is linked to the eyes. Stop it or you'll go blind when you are older!"

Three days later I am discharged, flushed from the sterile hospital bed back to our germ-hole of a flat with your Grand Mar. I don't want to leave these nurses, full of patience that your Grand Mar doesn't have, full of wisdom backed up by science

and proper training. Your Grand Mar just eyes them suspiciously, like she's the one with all the expertise and they are just
potty-emptiers.

"Look how young they are," she says. "As if any of them have
had their own babies. They've got all their training out of books."

Instead of calling your Grand Par to pick us up, your Grand
Mar calls a taxi.

"Why are you wasting money like this, Mah?"

"Your dad gave me fifty dollars to take you home," she tells
me. "He said he couldn't do it. He had some shit on, though
what could be more important than his own daughter and
granddaughter I don't know."

"Wow, brand-new baby," the taxi driver says to us when we
get in the car. He has a sleazy look I don't like at all. Five minutes into our trip, you start to cry. "You can feed him if you want.
I don't mind." He pauses, and when I make no move to follow
his suggestion, he tells me, "Nothing more beautiful than a nursing mother."

By now your Grand Mar has worked out that the driver is
dodgy, and this time I am relieved when she takes you. Your crying evaporates to a few hiccups.

"How old are you, love?" asks the driver.

"None of your business."

"You got a mouth on ya, don't ya?"

Yes, I think, if having a mouth means saying four words. But
at least it shuts him up.

When we arrive at our block of flats, your Grand Mar car-
ries you while I hold on to the stair rails. Fourteen flights, and
your Grand Mar tells me to stop every five steps. She doesn't

want my sinister Halloween scar down there opening up into a bloody grin.

I see the soft cotton cocoon your Grand Mar clutches to her chest, your head poking out the top. And I see how horribly hard our world is – the dangerous, gappy handrails, the narrow metal and dirty concrete, the dizzying drop to the bottom of the stairwell.

Never have I been so glad to see our front door.

Your Grand Mar has done something to the flat in the days I was in hospital. The coffee table has been pushed aside. All our couches have slunk to the corners of the room. It's as if every single thing we own now exists only to orbit the nucleus of your cradle, cartoon furniture bowing down before your arrival.

"Where'd you get the rocker from, Mah?" I ask. I thought she wanted you in our bed.

"Mrs Osman."

"She bought us a cradle?"

"She had one in her garage."

"But she doesn't have any children."

Your Grand Mar tucks you in carefully. "This cradle can be for daytime sleeps. At night she'll still sleep with us." I thought she'd changed the subject but she suddenly said, "She kept it for years. Not everyone is lucky enough to have a baby when they want, you know."

"Mrs Osman wanted a baby?" Those racing-car nails, that whoosh-cloud of hair. To me, she always seemed too fussy-glamorous for kids.

"And not every baby comes out alive," your Grand Mar adds. In the waxing room all those months, I thought that everything about your Grand Mar and Mrs Osman had dropped into the eaves of my prying ears, but now I realise I don't know Mrs Osman at all. I think about the times I was pissed off at her for wanting to pat my tummy, when she'd always been so nice to me. I feel a film of tears developing across my eyeballs, and try not to blink.

"Look at this," your Grand Mar exclaims, holding up a condom from the homecoming bag the hospital gave me. "They've chucked in whole handfuls! We can resell them."

"Do you even know what they are?" I ask her.

"I should ask you the same, since if you'd known about these you wouldn't have got pregnant in the first place!"

"Who are you planning to sell them to?"

"I'll send them back home to your aunties. They can sell them and take a cut."

Your Grand Mar makes a pile of nappy-rash cream and talcum powder samples. "We can send these back home too. Our baby doesn't need all this stuff. Just wipe her down with a cloth or wash her bum every time she does a poo." But she keeps the Johnson & Johnson baby shampoo and bath lotion.

That evening we have dinner in the living room, sitting on the floor while you lie on the sofa.

"We have to plan a party," your Grand Mar declares.

"But why?" I know she's in a good mood, but *this* good?

"In the past, most babies who were not strong died within the first month. So if they've made it through, it's a big cause for celebration."

Remembering what happened during my eighth birthday, and how I've never celebrated a birthday since, I feel only dread.

"Where will we have it?" I ask. "Dad won't come if it's here."

Your Grand Mar's face changes. "To hell with your father. This is my first grandchild. We're going to hold it at the May Hoa restaurant."

"That place is for full-on receptions! It's not a wedding, Mah." I'd been there once as a kid, and still remembered the ten-course banquet with shark-fin soup and the wedding cake with little bridges connecting each tier.

"We'll make him pay!" she says. "For not paying for my wedding reception. For not even having one, the cheapskate. We just had sandwiches and lamingtons in the foyer of the church. This time we'll have lobster and crab."

I wasn't allowed to eat crab under any circumstances when I was pregnant, even when we got rare leftovers of it from Siamese Please, because your Grand Mar said you'd be born with eleven fingers if I did.

"Okay, Mah, but you're the one who has to call him." I rummage through our clean laundry basket for a towel, in case she wants me to stay and help her plot perpetual revenge against your Grand Par.

"Where do you think you're going?"

"To take a shower."

"No you don't."

"What? Why? I took showers in the hospital. The doctor said I had to keep the cut clean."

"That was at the hospital. We don't do things like that. You can't shower or have a bath for a month."

She has to be joking.

She isn't.

If I wash my hair it will upset the energy balance, the chi, she tells me. Instead, your Grand Mar insists that I wipe myself down with washcloths steeped in a swampy-smelling Chinese medicine she's prepared. She even threatens to wash me herself, but I make such a fuss that she leaves me alone in the bathroom with the steaming brown bucket and washcloth.

"And remember not to squat," your Grand Mar yells through the door while I am sticking a maternity pad to a pair of fresh underpants. "You won't feel the effects of it now, but wait until you're older, when you find it hard to hold in your piss, and then you'll know what was good for you and who was good to you."

How am I meant to clean myself with this one small bucket? I dip the washcloth into the scalding hot herbal soup and wipe it across my arm. It actually feels good, but makes me smell like the drainage run-off from an ancient Chinese wet market.

"Hurry up!" yells your Grand Mar. "You've got to bathe quickly so you don't catch a cold. Stop dawdling."

Halfway through my scrubbing, while I am still squatting in the bathtub, the door bursts open and your Grand Mar barges in.

"I already have a towel, Mah!" I reach for mine to cover myself up, but she yanks it away.

"Dry yourself with this one, it's cleaner. I've boiled and dried it for you. I don't want you using ones washed with detergent chemicals." The towel she hands me is warm. I wrap it around myself and quickly pull on my undies.

"What's with this ridiculous privacy?" scoffs your Grand Mar. "There is absolutely nothing of yours I haven't seen. Now take that towel off because I've got to bind you." She holds out a long stretchy wad of material.

Before I have time to react, she's pulled off my towel and started wrapping the cloth tightly around my tummy. "Ow!"

"This will help you recover. It'll keep everything in place. And it'll help you lose the baby pouch faster." The binding is as uncomfortable as hell but she tells me I have to keep it on until bedtime, and then she'll bind me again tomorrow morning.

At breakfast I pour myself a glass of orange juice.

"No cold drinks!" she yells, yanking it away and replacing it with a steaming bowl. "These are the only liquids you need right now. Soups." She also won't let me eat bananas, coconuts, figs, rockmelons, watermelons. They are all "cold" fruits. I thought all fruits were cold, but if I don't follow her rules apparently I will have backaches, headaches and joint pains later in life. I can't even drink water from the tap.

She hands me a porcelain spoon.

I look down at the bowl and almost wet myself. A crinkly, deformed baby's hand is floating beside some peanuts, suspended in broth.

"What the hell is this, Mah?"

"Chicken's feet!" She looks at me strangely. "What's wrong with you? You've gone all white."

I don't say anything. I'm trying not to throw up or cry.

"Haven't you ever seen chicken's feet before? Of course not. You think meat comes in plastic trays at the supermarket. Those White Ghosts will have so much bad karma. They kill a chicken or duck just for its chest meat and thighs. Everything else they feed to their cats."

She also makes me soups of pig's trotters and peanuts, pig's stomach and papaya, and lots of boiled eggs – normal chicken eggs, not the abortive duck-foetus ones. I feel warmer after eating these meals, as if there's a little furnace in my centre radiating heat all the way to my fingertips and toes.

I had no idea that having a baby would fire up every cell in my body with such life and adrenalin. I want to be with you all the time, hold you all the time. You wouldn't cry so much if I could hold you, but your Grand Mar insists that I rest and not spoil you. She'll bring you to me if you need to be nursed because you prefer me to the bottle, which makes me secretly gleeful.

But time has stopped on our little island of bed, and I feel marooned. I swing my legs over the side.

"Aiyoh, don't get up!" yells your Grand Mar. "Whatever you want, I'll fetch it for you."

"I think Dad's magazine has arrived in the post. It comes around this time of the month."

"This is no time to be reading."

"Then what will I do?" I ask her.

"Just rest."

"No reading, no television? I am going to go mad!"

"How can life be so difficult for you? Maybe you're the one being difficult for life! All you have to do is sleep and eat, eat and sleep. Do you know how many girls would love to be in your position right now? Back home, girls gave birth and went back to work the next day because they had to."

She changes all your nappies, directing me to pass her talcum powder, safety pins and tissues moistened with warm water. She gives you your bath, ordering me to hand her the Johnson's baby shampoo, the facecloth, the water cup, the towel. She chooses all your clothes. I'm like a spectator to your life, a nurse to her doctor, passing her different instruments.

"Most people would be forever grateful to have a mother who does everything for them at this time," your Grand Mar tells me. "All you have to do is watch and learn. And yet you show me that dug-out-of-the-grave face again."

I can't help it. Because beyond your feeding, bathing and nappy changes, I am not allowed to be up. The worst thing is being forced to lie in bed like a sick person when I am so full of this feral vitality. No wonder all those ladies in Victorian-era novels were depressed and moribund. They couldn't walk around, work, play or anything. At least they could read, I thought resentfully. Mary Shelley and those sickly Brontë sisters even wrote entire books. Then I realise that those women all had dead mothers.

Keeping warm is very important to your Grand Mar, but in your first week of life, your nose mysteriously starts to run.

"See, I told you to keep her bundled up warm."

"She's too hot. It's stuffy in here, and she's wearing four layers!" I retort.

"That's just her natural healthy colour," she says. "All babies should have bright pink cheeks."

Then your nose is blocked. You try to feed from me but can't.

Your cries sound distant, like a radio recording of a baby with the volume turned down. Your nostrils whistle like a myna bird.

"Maybe she needs to see a doctor," I say anxiously.

"Nonsense." Your Grand Mar lifts you up to her face. She puts her mouth over your nose and sucks. I am horrified. Then she spits into the kitchen sink. "All cleared up," she says. "Now try feeding her."

I love you, but I am not sure that even I could have done that for you.

My gums start bleeding when I brush my teeth, so your Grand Mar urges me to stop brushing them altogether. "You'll make it worse and loosen them all!" she warns me. "Just rinse your mouth out with salt water." I ignore her advice, and close the door to the bathroom.

"Do you want all your teeth to fall out like mine did?" she hollers. "That's right, just ignore me. You wait until you're my age, and then you will know who was good to you."

I squeeze plenty of toothpaste on the toothbrush bristles, from end to end, like in the Oral-B ad. Brushing furiously, I look like a foaming, rabid Doberman in the mirror. At that moment, I think that maybe I should open up some of my stitches so I can go back to the hospital and be free of your Grand Mar for at least a few days. I can't even think straight when she's around. I'm just seething, snarling, defensive-angry all the time.

I *need* to get out of the house. What if it's an emergency, something she can't refuse? Then I have a brilliant idea. What if I *have* to see Dr Masano? Then I could tell her what is happening at home, and maybe she'll know what to do about your

Grand Mar. She wouldn't send me back home because I am on her books, her responsibility.

The next day, when your Grand Mar is outside hanging out clothes on the communal clothesline, I call the clinic.

"Can I please speak to Dr Masano?"

"I'm sorry, love, Dr Masano no longer works here," Kathy answers.

"What? But I'm her patient!"

"Love, she had lots of patients. She was a very popular doctor."

"But where's she gone?"

"Moved to another clinic."

"Do you know how I'd be able to find her?" I ask desperately.

"Dr Beam is her replacement, and I can assure you she's lovely."

I don't want Dr Beam, a stranger. I want my doctor!

"But I need to find Dr Masano." I need to tell her that my mother is keeping me prisoner in the house, with plans to steal my baby from me.

"Love, she's gone to the country. Bendigo. We have your medical rec—"

I hang up. The last time I saw Dr Masano was immediately after you were born. She'd walked over from her clinic to the hospital to visit us and give you a quick check-up. "She's perfect," she told me. "Well done, Karuna!" She told me that a nurse would be looking after us at the children's clinic, but never once mentioned that she would be leaving.

I wipe unexpected hot tears from my eyes. Fucking adults. I shouldn't be so surprised, this is the sort of shit they do all the time. I am the idiot, expecting a doctor to be there for me, for good.

Now there is no escaping your Grand Mar, no one to contradict her advice, no one to understand.

When she returns with the empty laundry basket, she looks at me closely. "Why are your eyes all red?"

"Mah, I need to see a doctor about my stitches," I tell her. "They hurt so much."

"The nurse checked your stitches. She said they were fine."

You suddenly sneeze and a clear bubble of snot inflates in one nostril.

"What about the baby?" I plead. "She's really sick. Look!"

"I told you to keep her bundled up but you keep peeling off her extra socks! We're not taking her to the doctor. Who knows what chemical crap they will put in her? She's too young for medicine. We just have to wait for the cold to clear up."

As your Grand Mar predicts, a few days later your cold clears. It is a happy day for me, but not for your Grand Mar, because that afternoon she gets a phone call from Mrs Osman.

After she hangs up, your Grand Mar fumes like a steaming kettle.

"Unbelievable! I told her I was taking the month off. I told her months and months ago! But she wants me to come back sooner! And I couldn't refuse because you know what she did? She started crying over the phone, saying how it was just her alone at the shop now, and how she couldn't hire another worker because she had to keep my job for me when I returned. Ha! Of course she has to – she'll never find someone as good as me. So I'll be going back next week, even though I have a newborn at home. But only because she was crying. That cunning bitch."

Inside I am soaring, but I do not make a sound, although I want to yell loud enough for all the flats to hear. I know that if I do, she'll take you away, claiming I've gone off my rocker, and you'll be gone from me, little cotton socks and all.

Now I just have to wait it out.

Chapter 14

When the day finally arrives for your Grand Mar to return to work, I am cow-jumped-over-the-moon ecstatic.

"I'm taking the key," she tells me in the morning, "because I know you will try to walk downstairs again. You'll bleed to death in the stairwell and no one will find out until I come home from work."

I don't care. A whole day without your Grand Mar is like a big, long exhale.

I hold you all day, and watch you make your old-man expressions and strangely loud noises. With your little furrowed brow and guarded face, those eyes moving from side to side to side, you look like a raw-faced declarer of Armageddon from an invisible pulpit outside the train station. Your grievances are many. When you open your mouth, your quivering petal of a tongue lists them in one pitch.

When you are asleep, I cut your fingernails. It is like defusing a bomb. Any little movement of yours sets me on edge. But I am a noiseless, patient spider, and eventually it's done.

"What's this rash on her face? It wasn't there this morning," your Grand Mar asks the first day she returns from work, pointing to your left cheek.

"She's just been nursing, with her face against my chest."

"I told you to give her the bottle."

I ignore her.

She takes you from my arms. "Ooh, my little baby," she coos, "Mar Mar missed you so much! Mar Mar was thinking about you all day today at work. Oo, what has your silly sister been doing to you today? Aiyoh, look." She points to your forehead. "That's definitely a scratch! How many times do I have to tell you to put mittens on her?"

"She doesn't need mittens. I cut her nails today."

"Aiyoh! Are you crazy?" She examines each one of your fingers. "Do you know how dangerous that is? What did you use?"

"The nail clippers."

"Oh, poor baby, look at your little fingers. Your silly sister has cut your nails too short and your fingertips are all pink now."

"Don't call me that. I'm not her sister."

She ignores me, and pops your whole hand into her mouth for a kiss.

The next evening, when she comes back, she exclaims, "Wah, her face looks thinner. Are you feeding her enough of that formula? Woo, my little precious pup. Look how small your face is! You sweet little puppy." She brings you close to her face and sniffs each of your cheeks. "Aiya, you are such a good baby. Let Mar Mar feed you now. Your silly sister has been starving you." She looks down at the coffee table. "What's the bottle doing there? You know you always have to put the leftover formula milk in the fridge. Are you trying to make her sick?"

"She doesn't like the bottle," I tell her. "She won't feed from it."

"Well, she takes it from me. Look!" Only a moment ago she was accusing me of poisoning you, and now she's shoved the same bottle teat into your open mouth, and your cheeks and chin move rhythmically around it. "See, look."

But you don't want the bottle when I'm around. You just want me. I am not your sister. A sister doesn't breastfeed her sibling.

The third evening, she orders me to put on the rice. "And I'll give this little doll a bath."

"You don't need to, Mah," I tell her. "I already bathed her this afternoon."

"What?" she cries. "I told you to wait until I come home to give her a bath. You have no experience! Babies are so fragile, one slip and you could drown her or drop her onto the floor and crack her head open and kill her."

"She's my baby and I can wash her."

"You just wait until something bad happens, then you'll be sorry."

"But she did a massive explosion in her nappy. It went all the way up her back, and almost reached her neck!"

"Pwoh. No wonder she stinks."

"I told you, I washed her. She doesn't smell."

"She does. Your silly sister didn't wash you properly, my pet."

I am about to have a massive explosion at the other end, but I clench my fists and keep my mouth shut.

Your Grand Mar whisks you away to give you another bath in the hand basin, leaving me to seethe. She has no idea about all the things I do for you in a day. She just comes home looking for the first thing to criticise, and always finds something. I can never do a good-enough job with you that she can't do better.

The next day, watching television, I start to notice all the things I am missing that would make me a better mother. Disposable nappies. Heinz baby food in little glass jars. A stick-mixer for pureeing applesauce. The ads teach me how to be a proper mum, and I realise I don't have the things to make that happen. As the TV yells louder, I feel the walls crowd in closer. I hold you tight, and sit unblinking and still.

I'm just a milk machine at the moment, I reassure myself. I don't need to get you stuff. All you need is right here. I just have to hold you and feed you. Hold and feed, feed and hold. Everything else I can put on hold.

I can't believe how long you sleep during the day, sometimes three- or four-hour stretches. I read. I write in my notebook. I watch television. I lounge around without feeling guilty. I make mugfuls of a sweet drink from a Salep Mix powder that Mrs Osman gave me to stir into milk.

At first, I don't think I am trapped like the first time, because all I can think about is how free I am, free of her presence. I have you all to myself and you are all I need. You fill up my hours to the brim. I sing to you, I make up stories. I show you *Fat Cat and Friends* on television.

Unlike the month when I was locked inside waiting for you to arrive and just wanted to sleep away the hours, now you give me so much to do. And I know exactly what to do with you because I have watched your Grand Mar do it for two weeks; standing by, fingers itching to pin that safety pin on the nappy, lather that shampoo into your dandelion scalp, button up the snap fasteners on your terry all-in-one.

The novels I'd once read about teenage mothers were always filled with crying babies who wouldn't settle, disgusting poo scenes that were meant to be funny, and young girls who hated being left alone with their kids. But I like being alone with you. Our days together are quiet, but the tranquillity ends the moment I hear your Grand Mar's key in the lock.

Your Grand Mar takes a day off work for your first visit to the nurse, when your cheeks and forehead are speckled with small red dots that not even she can diagnose.

"I will take her," your Grand Mar tells me. "You shouldn't be leaving the flat. You are still too weak."

"I need to get out, Mah! Look." I extend an arm. "I'm not getting enough sunlight. My skin's gone all white and sick."

"That's the colour it should be," says your Grand Mar. "Delicate."

I remember the words of the Goblin King. *Live without the sunlight, love without your heartbeat.*

"I'm sick of you taking over everything!"

"Fine," sighs your Grand Mar. "But don't say I didn't warn you when you collapse of exhaustion on the footpath."

Your Grand Mar dresses you in so many layers that your arms stick out like a penguin.

"What are you doing with that umbrella, Mah?" I ask when she grabs one from beside the door. "It's sunny outside."

"Exactly," says your Grand Mar, "I'm protecting her skin.

You don't want her to get any darker, do you?" She strokes your chin. "Poor baby, to be cursed with my skin instead of your silly sister's."

Your Grand Mar clutches her chest when we get to the bottom of the stairs. "Aiyoh, it breaks my heart that my daughter has to go out before the end of her month."

But I need to go with you, in case you are really sick and they take you to hospital. I need to be with you.

"You missed your first appointment," says Nurse Barbara when we arrive at her office. "We tried to call you at home but no one answered."

I shrug. What can I tell her? That your Grand Mar thought it was safer for me to stay in the flat with a bright-red newborn than it was to go and see a nurse?

"Has she got measles?" I ask.

"Oh no, those spots are just baby pimples. Don't rub anything on them – they'll go away on their own."

Nurse Barbara weighs and measures you, and you squirm madly like an upturned beetle. I start to fasten your nappy, but your Grand Mar slaps my hand away.

"You don't even have it folded properly yet!" she growls.

"She's doing a great job, Grandma," Nurse Barbara warns. "Let her have a go."

Your Grand Mar pretends she can't understand English again.

Very slowly and deliberately, I put your spotted jumpsuit back on. I cradle you and close my eyes.

"You poor thing," Nurse Barbara coos at me, "is the baby keeping you up? You're not getting enough sleep."

I smile because if I don't, your Grand Mar will say it looks like she's not looking after me properly.

Nurse Barbara points to the healthy foods pyramid chart. "Have you been eating your grains and cereals?"

"Yes," I say, still smiling. My face starts to ache, because when you don't feel like smiling you realise how many muscles it takes.

"Proteins?"

"I eat plenty of meat."

"Good. What about your vegetables?"

"Yes."

"What about fruit?" She points to the third layer of the pyramid, the most colourful one.

I remain quiet, because I know Grand Mar is shooting eyeball arrows at me. "No," I can't help confessing.

"Why not?"

"My mum thinks they're bad for me."

"Oh? Do you have allergies?"

"No."

"But it's summer – you should at least have mild fruit like watermelon, which is mostly water. You need to be well hydrated and keep your sugar levels up. You need energy to care for this little girl here. You poor thing, you look exhausted." Nurse Barbara rummages through her desk and brings out an orange Tupperware container. She peels open the lid. "Look. I have some left over from my lunch. Here!"

Rockmelon cubes, watermelon triangles, even a few cherries. I eye the watermelon.

"Do you want arthritis?" your Grand Mar warns in our language.

I withdraw my hand. "No, thanks, I'm okay."

Nurse Barbara is looking at me now, checking to see if I am *really* okay. "I'd like to talk to you alone, if I may."

Your Grand Mar glares at us both suspiciously.

"It's okay, Mum doesn't understand much English," I lie.

Nurse Barbara looks from me to Grand Mar, and then back to me again. "Alone, I'd prefer," she repeats. I dread your Grand Mar's interrogation afterwards, but I also feel a little cog of hope whir inside my chest.

"Tell that Ghost I won't be able to understand most of what she says anyway," your Grand Mar tells me, not getting out of her seat. When Nurse Barbara realises there is no way she can force your Grand Mar out, she ignores her instead.

"Are you okay?" Nurse Barbara asks.

"Yes, fine."

"I don't think you are, Karuna."

I start to cry. Shit!

I want to tell Nurse Barbara everything. Maybe she can help me. Anything would be better than this confinement.

But your Grand Mar's grip on me is stronger than love.

"I'll tell you what might help," Nurse Barbara says. "Perhaps you'd like to join a teenage mothers' group? You won't feel so isolated and alone. You might be able to make new friends and share tips and advice. It will get you out of home for a few hours, at least. They meet once every fortnight. Some of the girls are patients of mine. I think you'll really like them."

I am not sure whether I want to share you or my life with anyone else. I just want your Grand Mar to stop controlling me.

Nurse Barbara looks at her calendar. "The next meeting

should be in eight days' time at your local community centre. Would you like me to put your name down?"

"I dunno." I know for certain your Grand Mar won't let me go.

"Perhaps that might be too early. How about the following one?" She writes my name down on her calendar. "I'll follow this up with you, okay? I'll give you a reminder call a few days before, to see how you're doing."

Before we catch the bus back, your Grand Mar has to do some grocery shopping in town, which means I get to carry you. To my surprise, she buys a quarter of a watermelon and some pears. I almost cry with gratitude.

"I don't want you going to that mothers' group," your Grand Mar tells me as we walk from the bus stop back to our high-rise. "What can a bunch of teenagers teach you, huh? They're all in the same sorry place as you, have no clue what they are doing. All they've ever known is how to make mistakes, just like you."

She's so busy telling me this that we don't notice a grey car following us down the street like a slow-motion bullet.

"Oi!" the driver yells through his cranked-down window. He and his passenger are around your Grand Par's age.

"Don't look at them," your Grand Mar directs.

I clutch you closer to my chest, keep my head lowered.

"Oi! Youse!" the driver hollers. "Me love you long time!" There's laughter in the car.

"Fuck you!" your Grand Mar yells back.

"Ooh. Did ya hear that, Gareth?" the driver says to his passenger. "Two for the price of one. We get the Mama-san too."

I wish she'd just kept her mouth shut.

"Sucky sucky!" calls Gareth.

"Go to hell!" shouts your Grand Mar.

"Velly long time," hoots the driver. "Enter my Dragon!" They are not boys, they are men. As they speed off, their laughter is drowned out by their car's croupy cough.

Your Grand Mar turns to me. "Why do you shrink in the face of those shitheads?"

"I'm protecting the baby."

"If it weren't for me being by your side," she says, "things could have got nasty. You see, this is the exact reason why you should be a good girl and stay home. These streets are dangerous with animals like that on the loose."

She doesn't speak to me all the way home. She is probably angry that I was so embarrassed by her.

"You said you wanted it before!"

She slams the bowl of fruit on the table. Steam rises like fetid breath in a cold room. Your Grand Mar has wrung all the joy out of it, and the slimy warm pink mass reminds me more of a disembowelment than of fruit.

"When it was cold. I don't want *this*." Who the hell *boils* watermelon?

"You can't have anything cold," she hollers. "Do you want to damage your stomach and spleen?"

The way we do things, your Grand Mar always says, like there is No Other Way. When I ask why, she tells me that two thousand years of history cannot be wrong. And it's for my own good.

What are you doing in this country anyway, I want to yell, if nothing here is done the right way? If everything is wrong, why don't you go back to where you came from, where they're still having babies in wooden shacks, where nothing is sterilised except by boiling it in dirty river water, and where you won't be able to buy your beloved packaged food, all those frozen cheesecakes and Vienettas and Smith's chips?

"What a waste of my time and energy," your Grand Mar accuses.

Yes, I think, looking down at the ruined watermelon. What a waste.

Later that evening in bed I realise that you are one month old today. We didn't even have the party that your Grand Mar had been raving about all those weeks ago. I don't remind her, because what is there to celebrate?

Your Grand Mar turns to me. "Did you know those men who drove by and yelled at us?"

"No! They were Dad's age. Why would I know them?"

She is quiet for so long that I think she's fallen asleep. "Karuna," she says eventually, "if this baby came because of bad men like that, then you must tell me."

"Mah!"

"We are still keeping the baby. She's ours. But we could call the police . . ."

"Mah, no carload of morons came by and kidnapped me for an afternoon, okay?"

"You didn't yell back when they called us terrible things."

Because you were there, I want to reply, and you did the yelling for us. It's not as if this sort of stupid thing has never happened to me before. But now things are different. Now I am a mum holding a small baby and they are still bugging me.

The next night, when your Grand Mar comes home, I am watching television. I don't even pretend not to. I see a mum on a show carrying her baby strapped to her chest in a kind of harness. She's walking through bushland full of eucalyptus trees, and the baby looks very content, all his limbs pointing towards the ground like a ballet dancer coming down from a leap.

"Mah, can I get one of those?" Instead of being stuck to the baby – stuck inside a house, running towards your cradle whenever I hear grizzling – you'd be stuck to me, and I'd have my hands free.

"Don't be ridiculous. What are you, a monkey?"

"But my arms ache from carrying her too much." Every time I put you down, you wail like an alarm.

"Well, stop carrying her, you're only spoiling her," she scolds. "Just put her in bed or in the cradle."

"But the doctor says I should get some exercise during the day. I could go for walks with her."

"This is a very dangerous time for you. You shouldn't be going outside at all. If you're lonely, tell Tweezer to come over and keep you company and help you."

"Her parents won't let her see me," I say, "and she has to do work at home."

"See? She's a good girl, staying at home. If you were like her, you wouldn't be in this mess."

Home is driving me nuts. All I want is to get outside, use my legs, even just sit in the playground beneath our flats. But your Grand Mar insists I must not go anywhere. The way she sees it, every human being has already travelled far enough. Your Grand Mar says that people have many lives that stretch back through thousands of years, and if you are bad then you are reborn as a scorpion or snail or some trodden-on speck, but if you are good then you are born back in human form, into wealth, into comfort. "What kind of bad deed did I do in my past life," is her lament ever since I became a teenager, "to spend this one as a slave to an ungrateful child?"

I look at your face changing every few seconds with different expressions, like you're trying them all out, and think that maybe your Grand Mar's belief in reincarnation has something to it. Or maybe you are just practising all the feelings that you will feel in this life. When I see you, all foggy-eyed, trying to focus your gaze, trying so hard to look at the shitty world I have put you in, it breaks my heart. I think, what's the point? What's the point of trying so hard to see things when the things you will see are the things you will get so sick of seeing?

"Well, I'm going to get a pram," I tell your Grand Mar.

"How? You think the Salvation Army will come bearing this gift?"

I pull out your Grand Par's money from my pyjama pocket. I don't want to give your Grand Mar the chance to take my cash again, but I can't help it. I wave my one hundred bucks at her, like a red flag to a bull.

"I can get it myself."

"Where did you get that?"

"Dad. Who else?"

"Hand it over!" she says, extending her palm.

"No, it's mine. Dad gave it to me!"

"I'm the one raising you, and he hasn't given me a cent since he left. It's not yours. Don't be ridiculous."

"You don't get me the things I need."

"You don't need a pram!" she shrieks. "As if you could buy a pram for that amount anyway. How much do you think they cost?"

I have no idea, so I yell back, "You didn't even pay me for all that work I did for Mrs Osman."

"What do you call this?" She picks up your red stripey romper and three terry-towelling jumpsuits and throws them at me. "What do you call all these? I spend everything on you!"

"It's not for me, it's for *your* baby!" I holler back. "You've never let me have anything. Not even my own baby!"

"Hand it over," she says, quietly now, her hot, grasping hand extended again.

At that moment I hate her more than I have ever hated anyone in my life. I pick you up, shove you in her arms.

"Here," I yell, "have her!"

I bolt out of the room, ignoring her shouts. The key is hanging by a hook near the front door. I take it, pull the door closed and lock you both inside.

See how she likes confinement! Ha!

I stomp down the fourteen flights of stairs, ignoring the bee-stinging feeling of my stitches.

It is dark outside. The wire fence of the flats. The car park. The dirty plastic bags. The skip. Where can I walk to? What worse thing can happen to me? Slashing? Rape? Murder? At least I won't die in captivity.

The spring night might be unsafe but it is also empty. A dog barks and it sounds like a gunshot. The emptiness of nothing happening until something bad does. The emptiness of all the people caging themselves in their tiny flats to be safe. All sitting around, watching the news or yelling at each other over money, and sleeping back-to-back like opposing magnets. A match would crumble everything black.

I walk around the block. At first it feels good, this roaming. Let her think I have been killed or maimed. But then guilt pools in my stomach. She will be beside herself.

How silly. It's night-time. She's not locked in. She's in a warm flat with the spare key. The neighbourhood – if you can call it that, since we count no one our neighbours – is exactly the same in the dark. No more frightening or mysterious. The feral men who hollered at us from their car are probably at home tormenting their wives.

These are the streets that Ray and I cruised down. How dumb I was then to have thought it was freedom, what we had. Just because I was moving fast didn't mean I was moving away. He always, always drove in circles, and the larger they were, the more I believed we were going somewhere, but of course he always deposited me back here. Just like your Grand Par.

All I've done is lock myself away from the only two people who will miss me.

When I return, your Grand Mar is sitting on the couch, feeding you with a bottle. She glares at me. A steaming bowl rests on the coffee table.

Not the bloody watermelon again, I think. What a way to punish me.

Your Grand Mar puts your bottle down. She thrusts the bowl at me. "Eat this."

It's the warming soup made with ginger and chicken and little, bittersweet red-orange berries.

"And then feed her. She's starving. You've spoiled her – she won't drink from the bottle anymore."

Chapter 15

After my walkout, your Grand Mar doesn't say much to me. The only time she speaks is to give commands. By now, we've got an evening routine going. She cooks, I wash up. She bathes you, I feed you. On weekends she vacuums, I do the laundry. When you are asleep, we don't spend time together – for your Grand Mar, there is always something to be done around the house, or future meals to be made.

For me, there's this notebook to fill in. When I get your birth certificate, I will also hide it here. In fables, there is always a mother and there is always a daughter. There is sometimes a Grand Mar and sometimes a Grand Daughter. And the story that will be told to you, your whole life, is that your Grand Mar is your mother and you are her daughter, and I am your sister. But between the pages of this notebook, hidden away from your Grand Mar, you will find the truth. I'm keeping this record to let you know that it wasn't always that way. That you were once mine, and when I looked in your dark eyes, you made me very happy. I know I'm not an adult yet, and your Grand Mar can make all of my decisions and all of your decisions, but this is one thing she cannot take away from us.

I think about this life, the wasted hours, the unfairness of it all – to keep us, in rude, defiant health, locked up like this, like two pets scratching at the front door for Owner to come with small, packaged treats. And how small they are – sometimes, she brings home Smith's salt and vinegar chips, Haw Flakes, Vi-Va caramels, White Rabbit chews, Moonbits. She feeds us, she cares for us, she doesn't want a car to run over us. I should be grateful. Yet like an animal, I have no self-control. I devour the entire chip bag, or six Haw Flake rolls in one day. There is nothing to do, I have read everything in this house, even the junk mail. Sometimes when you are asleep I just sit there, stare into space and listen to the clock tick.

Even though it's not yet the end of spring, the days get hotter and hotter.

And you cry and cry and cry. Your veiny red leaf of a tongue quivers with fury.

And then nothing happens.

And nothing more happens.

I am back to feeling trapped inside, but I realise that this time it's much, much worse.

This time two of us are trapped.

Backward I see in my own days where I sweated through fog . . . I have no mockings or arguments – I witness and wait.

Even Walt Whitman is melting in the heat. His blue cloth jacket curls, and his spine cracks. He doesn't have long in this house, but at least Judith Wright is with him in his last days, she with her dead foxes and cut snakes.

I wish I could load up a pram like a magic carriage and escape. I'd fill it with nappies, some changes of clothes for both of us, some instant noodles and the money your Grand Par left me. But I can't. Like Tessa the homeless girl, we have nowhere to go. We'd be sent back home to your Grand Mar. She doesn't hit me, she doesn't hurt us – how would authorities see what is wrong with our situation?

But I am not sure we're going to survive the summer, with the mercury already rising so fast.

It rises every single day, and soon the day comes when the mercury rises high enough to paint the ceiling silver, and we are still inside.

"Help me." I bang on the front door, but I know that our next-door neighbours, the Petcevics, will be at work at the Kinnears rope factory, and that those above and below me couldn't care less.

I pull all your clothes off, unpeel your nappy. Your skin is slimed like a milky fig, your face a frenzy of magenta. I put you to my boob but you turn your head away and wave your limbs like an upturned slater.

Shit, shit, shit.

I unspool our casement windows as wide as they can go, which leaves only a twenty-five-centimetre gap. They were designed this way to stop the suicides. I see the air treacling with heat. The outside world looks like one of those warped funhouse mirrors. It is futile to chuck a note out the window – most of the people in our block can't read, and even if they could read they wouldn't pick up a scrap of paper on the ground.

I yell at the top of my lungs, "Help, help! It's so hot and I am trapped here! My mum's locked me inside with my baby, help! Help!"

Not a flutter at any window, nothing. I could be stabbed to death in the flat and no one would blink an eye.

I limp to the phone to dial 000. What a stupid number, I think, as I wait for the round dial face to *click, click, click* back before dialling the next 0. A person could die of suffocation before the dial rotates back.

"Fire, police or ambulance?" asks a female voice on the other side.

"I'm suffocating."

"Is there a fire on the premises?"

"No, my mum has locked me in the house."

"Police, then."

"No!" I shout. "NO! My mum has locked me and the baby in the flat while she has gone to work and I'm suffocating."

"Where are you locked?" she asks. "In a confined space? Cupboard? Where are you calling from in the house?"

"Just the phone," I say. "But it's so hot. And I can't get out. I just need someone to come and unlock the door."

"You want someone to unlock the door?"

"Yes!"

"Who has the keys to the flat?"

"My mum."

"Does she have a phone at work?"

"Yes."

"Why don't you call her at work? Tell her to come home immediately and unlock you."

I pause. What can I say?

"How old are you?" she asks, suddenly suspicious.

"Sixteen! I'm sixteen."

"You don't have a key? Call your mother!"

"No, you don't get it, I can't – she was the one who locked me in here in the first place, I keep telling you."

"We need to notify the police. They can come and get you."

"No!"

"Are you being held against your will? Can you breathe?"

Shit, the police will come and break the locks! They will take us and lock away your Grand Mar. And I will be the cause of all this.

"What is your address, please?"

"Look, I can call my mum," I say.

"What is your address?" she repeats.

"No. No, it's okay." I hang up.

I stagger to the bathroom with you in my arms and open the window. I rinse a facecloth under the cold tap, hold your body in the washbasin and cover you with the cloth, like a little blanket. Your colour subsides, your howling turns into small hiccups. You are cooling down.

Phew.

Carrying you to the kitchen, I yank open the fridge and freezer door. I pull up a vinyl chair and sit there directly in front of the *Frigidaire* with you in my arms, not caring about the icicles that will form or the milk that might sour or the meat that might rot.

That evening when I hear your Grand Mar's key turn in the door, I stand by, waiting. The moment she walks in, face bright red, dishevelled, breathing like a thirsty dog, I start.

"We almost died! We almost died because you locked us in! Feel how hot it is now! It was even hotter this afternoon."

"Alright, alright, stop your hollering," she tells me. "Stop blowing things up. You didn't die. Plenty of people were in their flats at the same time, and I don't see any ambulances out the front."

But the next day after work, she puffs up the fourteen flights of stairs hauling a large, heavy box. She sets it in the middle of our living room.

"I'll hold the baby while you put it together," she tells me. "There's a box of your dad's tools in the spare room."

It's a pedestal fan with a rotating head and three settings. The fan sits in the middle of the living room while we have dinner, its head slowly moving from side to side as if disapproving of this life of ours.

With the new fan, I improve my makeshift air-conditioner. Instead of leaving the fridge and freezer doors open, I tie an empty ice-cream container in front of the fan's wiry cage. As the day gets hotter, I fill it with ice cubes, and we sit in front of it.

When the new edition of *Reader's Digest* comes, I cling to it like a bible, because it has twenty-two new stories in it, which means twenty-two new voices talking to me, twenty-two new people to keep me company, twenty-two wholesome folk who speak in full sentences, unlike that crazy, cracked, skinny-dipping Whitman.

We accept true inspirational stories of up to 500 words, the editor writes on page three. There is nothing inspiring about my life, unlike the neurosurgeon they profiled this month, or the heroes who stopped a plane from crashing. Even the tragic stories always yield some lesson about resilience. Positive thinking and gratitude, the *Digest* tells me, are the keys to happiness. I do not feel it. I do not believe it. But I want the two hundred bucks they pay for a story.

Being a teenage mother was not something I planned, I write in my blue biro. *But things were not going so well at home, with my dad leaving and my mother always trying to control everything I did and everywhere I went. One day a nice boy pulled up in a silver car and gave me a ride. I returned the favour, except I didn't have a nice silver car.*

I spend four days on these five hundred words, in between your feeds and sleeps. Reading back over it, my story sounds like it belongs to another girl, one whose mother works two jobs to support her, who keeps her inside to protect her from marauding gangs and racist hoons. One whose mother sounds loving and reasonable, not mean and paranoid.

Retrieving my stamp from Whitman's jacket pocket, I stare at the two ginger boys on it and wonder if you'll ever get a chance to have a Great Australian outdoors childhood or whether the only yabbies you'll see will be on television. There is no glue in the house, because your Grand Mar didn't want me using it when I was pregnant. "Using sticky stuff will cause the baby to have birthmarks," she had warned. I make some cornflour paste for my stamp, and press it on a homemade envelope tenderly, like a kiss on a baby's cheek. Then I put my story back in the care of Whitman, until such time as I am able to feed it into the wide, accepting mouth of an Australia Post box and see if my fake life will take flight on the wings of the *Reader's Digest* Pegasus.

*

A few days later, as I am nursing you, I hear four sharp knocks.

I look into the fish-eye lens of our front door and see two strangers' faces stretched out.

"Department of Community Services. Open the door, please."

"I don't have the key."

"Does anyone at home have the key?"

"No."

"We are going to come in, okay? My name is Erika and I have my colleague Yiannis with me. We're going to get the master key from the administrator of the flats, and then we are coming in."

I didn't even know there was a master key to the flat.

"Nah, it's okay. All is good here and my mum will be home soon."

"Is it alright if we visit for a little bit?" Erika asks, but I know it is not a question. I don't know what to do, so I stay silent. I hear their footsteps retreat.

In the fifteen or so minutes it takes them to return, I panic, and the panic makes me useless. I decide to clean the flat, but there is not much I can do while holding you in my arms, and besides, the flat is already tidy. I keep picking up objects with one hand – a cheese grater, a jar of soy sauce, a supermarket catalogue, one of your squeegee toys – and putting them back down in the same place.

I hear the key turn in the lock.

I stand with you in my arms like a fat shield. "Hello," I say. "Come in." But they have already let themselves in.

The two community service workers sit down on our couch, and Erika says, "Come join us," as if this is their house. I sit on the couch opposite, and they lean forward and fuss over you, chucking your chin, exclaiming at your strong grip, stroking your round knees. I know they are checking for bruises, and they won't find any.

I realise I should offer them a cup of coffee, but we don't even have that here. Your Grand Mar doesn't trust me not to drink it. She's scared it will go into my milk and you'll be an insomniac. We must look like such tight-arses.

"One of your neighbours called us, said that your mother was keeping you locked in the house with a newborn baby," says Yiannis. "They heard you yelling out the window. Is this true?"

So someone *had* heard me. "She was only locking me in to keep me safe."

"Safe from what?"

How can I explain the craziness that is your Grand Mar to these people? Safe from the world?

"Where is your father?"

"He left us two years ago."

"What if there is an emergency with your baby?" Erika asks.

"Then my mum told me to call her at work. Or to call emergency."

Where would you go with a new baby anyway to get help? your Grand Mar scoffed. *Take the bus one hour to the hospital? Better they come with their ambulance, smash the door down.*

"Is there anyone else, besides your mum and emergency services, that you can rely on?"

I remain silent.

"Are you a danger to your baby or yourself?" Yiannis asks.

"No!"

"I'm sorry," Erika says more gently, giving Yiannis a glare, "but that's a question we have to ask. I can see you're doing a very good job. Baby looks well cared for and happy." She doesn't offer to pick you up, because she can see that I will never let you go. "What does your mother do?"

"She's a hairdresser."

"When does she usually come home?"

"In about an hour." It was close to five, and I knew she would be sweeping the floor now, packing away the scissors and hair dryers. "She catches the bus back."

"Does she understand English?"

"Yes. A bit."

"And you're here all day, until she gets home?" Yiannis asks.

I can't lie, although I want to. I see the two of them look at each other. Then they don't say anything more, just continue looking around our house from the couch. I know they've probably seen the innards of some of the flats around here: rooms filled with rotting nappies and decaying food, clear signs of neglect and horror. Our house is neat and clean, just as you are.

Erica spots the photo of me as a baby. It's a bit hard to miss, considering it takes up most of the wall. She smiles. "Is that you?"

"Yes."

"What a gorgeous baby."

You start to grizzle.

"You need to feed her," says Erika, as if I don't already know, but I don't want to do it in front of those two.

"Why don't you pop into the bedroom? Don't worry, we'll be right here," she says, even though that's exactly the reason I am worried.

I take you to our bedroom and close the door.

I have fantasised about this moment for so long – how your Grand Mar would no longer be able to put one over the community service workers, unlike the time at Christ Our Saviour with her good grooming and manners. This time I would be ready, I'd talk over her if I had to; I'd tell the truth. I would make them see sense. I would tell them that not only was your Grand Mar locking me inside all day, but she was forcing me to live a lie.

Yet while I am nursing you, I think about your Grand Mar taking those two weeks off to boil me soups and bathe you and put lotion on your skin when you had a rash, and even sucking the snot out of your nose when you had that cold. I think of her working overtime for weeks beforehand, of her going out and buying me the special food that radiates heat, of how she even cut my toenails when I couldn't bend over. I think of how I can sleep at night – even when I don't want to – because any time you make the slightest *eheheh* sound she will rock you back to sleep. I think about how your Grand Mar has got you everything you own that's not donated.

I look down at you, a little animal with unfocused eyes solely concentrating on sucking milk from me. How easy you are to satisfy. You're all needs, and no wants yet.

Your Grand Mar may not give a toss about my wants, but she tries to meet all my needs. She provides for me, she cares for me, she does things that she thinks are for my own good. This is what she knows to be love – a verb, not a feeling. And as much as I hate to admit it, she meets all your needs too.

I am afraid now in a new way.

Very afraid.

When you are done, I return to the living room and sit with the two intruders, who are busily writing things down on clipboards. Erika smiles at me, but Yiannis doesn't look up.

An eternity later, I hear your Grand Mar's key turn in the lock. Erika and Yiannis don't notice this sound because, unlike me, they haven't been tuned in to it for months. So they first hear her voice: "I brought home a box of lamb kebab. Mrs Osman roasted it. Have you put on the rice cooker yet?" She enters the lounge room sweating, her yellow T-shirt flecked with hair dye, her blue polyester trousers crumpled, her hair falling out of a rubber band. She sees me first, then notices our visitors.

"Hello?"

"Hello, Mrs Kelly," Yiannis says, standing up. "We're from the Department of Community Services. We're here to help."

Your Grand Mar looks at me. "Your teachers?" she asks.

"No, community service workers," I reply in English. She has no idea what they are. "Government people," I tell her in our language.

I see the same fear I feel mirrored in her face.

"Hello, Mrs Kelly," says Erika, smiling. "Please sit down with us."

But your Grand Mar doesn't sit. She stands by the doorway, blocking it. I know that she is thinking that at the end of this visit, one or both of us may be gone.

"What's happening?" she asks. "Is my dawtah in trouble?"

"Well," begins Yiannis, "yes. Or she could be, if she doesn't have a way to leave the flat." They explain the risks of fire and emergency to her, this woman whose whole heart is filled with fire and emergency.

"Why do you lock her up?" asks Erika gently.

"Keep her safe when I go working."

"But how *old* is she?" asks Yiannis.

"Sixteen."

"Old enough to be a mother," he tells her. "Old enough to be responsible for another human being. So old enough to make decisions for her baby. Decisions to keep her safe."

"But she doesn't know how —" begins your Grand Mar.

Yiannis cuts her off. "See here?" he says, pointing to his clipboard. "Your daughter, on the hottest day this month, made a call to emergency services. It's registered here. She felt that her baby was in danger. She knows how to act responsibly."

Your Grand Mar stares at Erica and Yiannis with eyes like a hunted badger's.

"Come, please, sit down with us," says Erika, beckoning.

Your Grand Mar finally drags her feet over and sits next to me, back hunched over. I feel her heat and smell the chemicals on her clothes.

"I single mother," she tells Erika, "so hard. I work two jobs. Day time salon cutting hair and night time cook at Thai restaurant."

Erika nods sympathetically.

Your Grand Mar points a shaking finger at me. "She have baby and the boy run away. I never even see him. She won't even tell me who is he."

Then your Grand Mar starts to cry! Big, heaving, honking sobs. She doesn't even bother wiping her face. "She hard to control."

I can't believe it. She still wants to blame me, even for my imprisonment. I don't feel at all sorry for her right now, because

I can see how this looks to the community service workers –
her wild daughter getting herself knocked up by some scum in
the commission flats, sly and secretive, while this hardworking
migrant mother is at the end of her tether looking after them all.

Erika leans towards her. "We understand," she says.

Stupid Erika *doesn't* get it at all. In fact, Yiannis, the one
I was first wary about, the one who seemed so judgemental,
is the one who seems to see how wrong all this is. I want to
tell him that your Grand Mar is trying to steal you away from
me and make you hers alone. Before I can open my mouth to
yell out the universal lament of all teenagers – *you just don't
understand* – your Grand Mar pinches my upper arm and
hisses at me in our language, "Shut up. Do you want them to
take the baby away? Do you want them to lock me up?"

And she has voiced it, our greatest fear. What would I be,
and where would I be, without both of you? No one to love me,
no one to love. Nothing, nobody, nowhere.

"What is she saying?" Yiannis asks, his brown hawk-eyes
never missing a thing.

Your Grand Mar is still glaring at me, but I translate for him,
word for word.

"No one is getting locked up," Erika says gently, "but we
need to make sure Karuna and her baby are safe. And she's not
safe locked up at home."

"You have to trust your daughter," Yiannis adds. "You have
to trust that she is old enough to make decisions for herself and
the welfare of her child."

Your Grand Mar looks down at our tattered floor rug and
doesn't say anything, so Erika continues.

"We recently saw a boy, eight years old, whose dad had to work and left him in the flat by himself all school holidays. He turned on the stove to cook an egg and got pretty badly burned by boiling water. Luckily he was smart enough to call 000. You can't lock your daughter up. It's dangerous. She needs her own key."

"I took it because she stealing from shops. Downstair milk bar. When she by self, she get into trouble. At home, she good girl. She clean. She cook. She help me a lot."

"We'd like to see her have her own key, please. As a safety precaution," says Yiannis.

Your Grand Mar finally opens up her battered blue hand-bag. She pulls out the spare key to the flat. A tiny piece of metal, no bigger or more valuable than a couple of coins, and yet – the power it has held over me for months! I am so surprised that I forget to put out my hand, and it drops to the carpet. Your Grand Mar makes no effort to pick it up.

Because I am still carrying you in my lap, Erika bends over, picks up the key and places it in my palm.

I put it in my shirt pocket and it burns a hole of shame there.

I have forced your Grand Mar, in front of these adult strangers, to hand over her control.

"We'll do a friendly visit in a few weeks' time," Yiannis says to me. "Just to see how the three of you are going."

There is nothing friendly going on after they leave. The quiet is the quiet following a massacre. When she's sure they are well and truly gone, that they aren't going to barge back in to bust her, your Grand Mar stands over me and starts shouting, "Why do you do this to me?"

I clutch the key in my pocket and you in the other arm. "Because you are trying to kill us."

"I'm trying to protect you!"

"In a way that will kill us."

"What is so dangerous about being at home?" she shrieks. "All your food is prepared – all you have to do is heat it up. You can spend the whole day in bed. You don't have to go to work. You're not supposed to do anything except keep that baby fed and alive. And you still do this to me!"

"I yelled out the window the other week because we nearly died – it was hell in here."

"But I got you the fan, didn't I?"

"I didn't know that the government people were coming. Some neighbour must have dobbed us in."

"Because of you!"

This is true. But it is also true that your Grand Mar isn't entirely innocent.

"No," I retort, "because of *you*. You are the one who locked us in."

"And what's so good about going outside, huh? What is there out there? A parking lot where you can get run over? A row of factories you might want to work in? Dangerous hoons who follow you in their cars? A bloody school that no longer wants you? Tell me, what is there outside that you want to see so badly?"

There is a library, for starters, that I know does story-time sessions for children. I'd seen the posters when she still took me to borrow books, before my confinement. There is the community centre. There is even the park beneath the flats. But of course, I can't tell her any of this. She won't let me read in case I go blind. How can someone so ignorant have such complete control over my world and its boundaries?

"You don't know anything!" I rage. "You are turning us into dumb animals!"

Her hands are trembling fists. Her face is a mad magenta. "You're right!" she rails. "They're right! I don't know anything!" She's like a big baby overflowing with futile fury, a grown-up, upright replica of you before you howl.

"No, you don't," I say, rubbing it in. "You can't lock me up to keep me safe."

And there and then, I have said it. Love is not all about control, despite what your Grand Mar believes.

"You can't keep me locked up to keep me safe," I repeat, the same way Sarah repeated *You have no power over me* to Jareth the Goblin King, over and over, until he was nothing but scrappy rags that blew away when the night wind passed. "You've had your go. You can't have a second shot, even if you think you've stuffed up. She's *my* baby!"

Now your Grand Mar starts to cry. But this time, it is not the sort of crying she'd put on for the community service workers. This time it is noiseless and still, her mouth contorted into an infinity sign of suffering.

She comes to sit next to me, and I feel horrible for not wanting her near, but it's the truth. I don't want her near you either – I don't want her grabbing you from me. You're just a baby, you're not supposed to comfort my tantruming mum; just as I never knew what to do with her aching loneliness after the divorce.

"Everyone can see that she's my baby!" I say. The social workers, Nurse Barbara, the midwife at the hospital. "Why can't you?"

"She's not going to be this way forever, you know," your Grand Mar says quietly. "She'll learn to talk. She'll learn to walk. She'll answer back to you. She'll run away from you. How are you supposed to control her? You're still a child yourself."

Your Grand Mar wipes her eyes with her sleeve pulled over her fist, the way a little child does. "As a baby, I was looked after by my grandma. All babies needed back then was a little triangle kerchief for a top and bare bums in the sun, three bowls of rice porridge a day. If they were lucky, some Nestlé sweetened condensed milk mixed with water. My grandmother loved me but my own mother let me run around like a beggar's child and didn't care if my hair was a seaweed basket or if buttons fell off my shirts. She let me roam in the streets between parked cars and scrape my shin open on a metal stairwell. She didn't give a shit because she was always busy working, selling boiled eggs and banana desserts in the market, and I wasn't the precious, beautiful one like my sister Lee Lee."

Your Grand Mar tells me about the children she saw in the marketplace in her old country, standing next to their cold-eyed parents, being sold as domestic slaves – a life better than the one their own folk could offer, one with regular meals and shelter from the night. About a boy who broke his arm, and when it healed it stuck straight out, locked at the elbow. A girl who realised she was blind in one eye only when she couldn't see through a little kaleidoscope toy that a White Ghost had given her – she had thought that everyone used only one eye.

"The world is a dangerous place for children who are unloved, unwatched and uncared for. Children with no one to claim them. You were born into a world far away from the dirt-poor Tsinoys of my old neighbourhood. Being poor can make a person wild. I just don't want you to become wild. I don't want our baby to either."

When I still don't look at her, she stands up and shuffles into the kitchen. I can hear her turning on the tap to rinse the rice, turning on the oven to warm up the lamb. I know she'll also boil the kettle so that she can prepare some formula for you. She's missed the start of her shift at Siamese Please, because when the phone rings and she answers, I hear her trying to convince Yenny that she's suddenly fallen ill with food poisoning.

I feel the hard-clenched fist of anger in the centre of my chest, the fist that was ready to strike out at her, loosening.

We have a late dinner, and we're so exhausted that we end up sleeping on the floor of the living room with the pedestal fan on, like geckos curled around your cradle.

Chapter 16

That social worker visit and our blow-up shifts something in both of us. I know that outsiders see us as two separate people, and now your Grand Mar knows that they are willing and able to cleave us apart. Although she's livid about what I've done, now she knows I can do things even in this cramped flat, things to bring in interference and help.

So the key stays with me now. Your Grand Mar does not ask for it back the next day, or the day after that, or the next week.

The first day, I carry you downstairs and walk around the park so you can look at the trees, their canopy of eucalyptus leaves. So you can see the right-angled and triangular shapes of the children's play equipment, the way the light turns them into solid beams and shadows. You are so stunned that you barely cry. The next day I do the same. The day after, we go for a walk around the block. I take it slow, like a sick person recovering from lying down all the time. You are now seeing something other than the ceiling. You marvel at the sky.

In the evenings, your Grand Mar returns. When she asks what we did, I tell her the truth. We walked to the postbox to post a letter. We walked to the park. We walked around the block.

"Don't go too far," she says. "There are people who might

snatch her away from you." I tell her I can't go too far anyway – only as far as my arms can hold you up. "And watch out for cars," she adds. Ha, I think, too late: a car – a lovely, silver car – is how I got myself into this mess.

Because we've not had any way to mark your arrival, I walk you to the community centre. This is where it all started, I tell you. The place is as quiet as ever, but miraculously, there is some- one at the front office.

"I'm here for the young mothers' group," I lie. "I think it's in one of the rooms at the back." Before the receptionist has a chance to ask any questions, I breeze on through. It is amazing the things I can get away with, carrying you as an excuse.

Of course, I am sussing out whether there are any more free books, since I haven't been to the library for so long, and it's too far for us to travel on the bus just yet. There's a room at the end of the hallway, a few doors down from the Homework Help room, that I hadn't noticed before. It's completely empty – there aren't even any tables and chairs. Like the Homework Help classroom, there are very old posters tacked on the wall, and a poem. I walk up to take a closer look. *Your children are not your children*, I read.

This is not Whitman, but it is as if an uncanny power is speaking to me.

> *They come through you but not from you. And though*
> *they are with you, yet they belong not to you.*
> *You may give them your love but not your thoughts, for*
> *they have their own thoughts.*
> *You may house their bodies but not their souls, for their*

souls dwell in the house of tomorrow,
Which you cannot visit, not even in your dreams.

The Blu Tack is so old it's almost melted the poster onto the wall, but I pull it down carefully and roll it up. The young receptionist doesn't even acknowledge me as I walk out with my ill-gotten gain.

The community service workers return for their follow-up visit. Your Grand Mar dangles the two sets of keys in front of them – hers and mine. She tells Yiannis that I am going for walks every day downstairs, in the park beneath the flats. She even lets Erika hold you for a little bit. She tells them she will quit one of her jobs to mind you next year, so that I can go back to school. "My daughter is very smart," she says, "smarter than me. She will study business one day."

"Come to Mar," your Grand Mar coos to you every evening, "we're going to have a great time together when your sister goes back to school," and I am reminded that I will soon be separated from you, that soon her role and mine will reverse. She will have your days while I have your nights.

During our walks, I sometimes see other teen mothers wheeling their prams like they are full of rocks. I hear one scream at her grizzling baby, and another rant to her friend about how she got kicked out of home. At our last check-up, Nurse Barbara had asked if I had a strong support network, which I imagined to be a cluster of best friends, aunties and babysitters who could hold my baby, listen to me vent over the phone about scrambled-egg poo and organise play dates. The sort of stuff you see on television.

But now I realise what it actually means. Your Grand Mar is my sole support network – she has to be all those people. If she were your father, I would be bitterly disappointed by the lack of sweetness, of romance, even of civility; but because she is my mother, I put up with her finite, roaring, ferocious self. I know for certain that your Grand Mar might lock me up, but she would never, ever kick me out. It is never a problem that your Grand Mar doesn't care enough for us. The problem with your Grand Mar is that she *cares too much*.

But day by day, I notice small concessions. Just the other evening I put ice cubes in my water and she didn't say anything about me damaging my spleen. I turned on the television and watched an episode of *Neighbours* while nursing you and she didn't switch it off or turn it to the news. The next evening she even brought home some yoghurt. "This is supposed to be good for your bones," she told me.

When you are sleeping one Sunday afternoon I take a shower, still expecting to be interrupted at any moment. When your Grand Mar doesn't appear, I stay longer, adjusting the water until it's cool enough to raise goosebumps. Turning off the shower, I expect her to barge in with her binding cloths, but she doesn't.

I take my time getting dressed and think, finally, she's giving me some privacy.

I exhale.

Finally my body feels like my own again, and I can start having some time to myself.

Things are getting better, I think. Slowly but surely.

I enter the living room and see your Grand Mar holding your face very close to hers, her neck bent, head lowered. The affection she lavishes on you always comes as a surprise to me. Who knew she could be so doting?

Happy-groggily, I assume that she's stroking your cheek – until I see the glint of metal.

"What the hell are you doing, Mah?" I yell without really thinking, rushing towards you.

"Aghh!" she screams in surprise.

A small gap of silence, and then the worst sound of all: you start to wail, but it's not your usual waking-up wail.

It's a raw cry of shock and pain.

"Give her back to me NOW!" I yank you out of her arms, and watch in horror as a line of tiny red pearls bead beneath your left eye.

"Aiyoh, now look what you made me do!"

"Me?" I roar. "Me?! I'm not the one who stabbed her with a pair of scissors!"

"Is she hurt?" Dropping the nail scissors on the coffee table, your Grand Mar leans over to take a look and sees the blood running down your cheek. "Aiyoh! Give her to me!" She holds out her arms, but I push her away. "You scared me!" she accuses, "if you hadn't come barging in, yelling —"

"Shut up," I warn. "You did this to her. You cut *my* baby." I swipe your cheek with my sleeve.

"Stop that! Your sleeve is dirty, you'll give her an infection. I'm going to get some cotton balls."

I have to sit down because I am shaking with such terror and rage. Your Grand Mar comes back and tries to wipe your face but I snatch the cotton balls from her trembling fingers.

"You're not touching her. What were you doing – trying to kill her? What is wrong with you, Mah?"

After I wipe away the blood, I see with relief that it is just a scratch.

"I was cutting her eyelashes."

"What the hell?"

"So they'll grow back longer and thicker."

She who wouldn't let me bathe you or cut your nails because it was too dangerous and I wouldn't know what I was doing! She who wouldn't let me shampoo your head in case I accidentally pressed too hard! Then I look down and notice it: tiny clumps, soft and short like the hairs of a mouse, scattered on the carpet. I pull off your knitted cap to confirm my suspicions. "You cut off all her hair too!"

"Yes, this is the best time to do it, when they are asleep and too small to move much or let their hands get in the way. If you hadn't scared me —"

"Shut up! *You* did this!"

"I did the same to you, and it worked, didn't it?"

"For God's sake, Mah! It's called genetics. You get these things from your parents."

"Yes, you got it from me because I was smart enough and careful enough and loved you enough to do this to you when you were a baby." Then, as if I were denying you something important, she demands, "Don't you want your daughter to be beautiful?"

"No," I retort, "it doesn't matter to me. She was born perfect and you're the one ruining her. You risked blinding her so that she could blink at boys! You do this sort of shit again and I'm calling the government people. Last time I didn't mean to, but this time I will."

"Oh, so you're *sooo powerful* now," jeers your Grand Mar, "because you have that phone number. Stop exaggerating. It was all safe until —"

"— *your silly sister came in and scared me. It was all good until your silly sister interfered,*" I spit. "Mar knows best. Mothers always know what's best for their babies. Well, she's not yours, Mah. *I'm* the mother. This is *my* baby. I know what's best for her and it's not this!"

"Fine, if you think you are so smart, why don't you look after her all by yourself and see how far you get?"

I am terrified because there are so many things I am still uncertain about. Half the time, I don't know whether I am doing the right thing with you. I think of that story in the Bible, the Judgement of Solomon, where two women are fighting over a baby and the king tells them that the only way to resolve it is to cut the baby in half. The real mum panics and says that the other woman can keep the baby.

If I assert myself as your mother now, then I must step up as your mother forever, and not stand aside as your sister, no matter what your Grand Mar calls me – or tells you to call me – in the future.

I know I have to do this. The fear is there, but my love is stronger than fear.

"You're not doing anything like this to my baby ever again," I warn her. "And if you try to make one more excuse, I will pick up the phone and call the government people to come back immediately. I don't care what happens after that. If you want to look after her, you do it as her grandmother. *I'm her mother.*"

She has no words.

And I know that your Grand Mar's love is greater than her anger, because she doesn't tell me to take you and leave, to get out. She just stands there, squeezing some cotton wool, staring woefully at the little nick beneath your eye.

I comfort and shush you and put you back in your cradle.

Finally, standing up, I ask, "Did your grandma – the one who looked after you – make you call your mother your sister?"

Of course your Grand Mar doesn't reply, because the one adult in her life who loved her unconditionally never made such a demand.

Chapter 17

Your Grand Mar has a sense of grudging respect for me now, a respect so new and so undeveloped that its mole eyes are still searching for signs to burrow underground again. Maybe she understands that, just as she wants to protect me, I want to protect you. I don't ask her, because there's a lot we don't say to each other. I occasionally still hear her calling herself your "Mar" but at least she doesn't refer to me as the silly sister anymore. At least, not in my presence.

We still have our flare-ups, of course. The other day she wanted to bottle-feed you cooled boiled water but I wouldn't let her. "Nurse Barbara says babies only need breastmilk," I told her. "If you think she's hot, then just take off one of her three layers of clothes." She hmphed but peeled off your cardigan. She also suggested taking me to an acupuncturist to deal with the tiger-stripe stretchmarks on my belly, but I told her to lay off. "I'm just looking out for you," she grumbled, "for your future. Don't you want to get married one day? Do you think a man is going to want to be reminded —"

"That I have a kid?" I answered back. "Well, I hope so, because my baby isn't going anywhere without me."

Your Grand Mar knows I am still wild, not tame, and she has had to accept this. After all, I went ahead and created a new life without her.

"I know we didn't have the one-month celebration," she tells me one Sunday afternoon when we are folding laundry. In fact, it's been more than three months since your arrival. "We can celebrate your baby's first one hundred days of life instead."

Now I wonder if she is just making it up as she goes along, this cultural thing. But that doesn't stop me noticing her words: *your baby*.

"Better we were cautious and didn't celebrate too early," she says.

We didn't celebrate any earlier because we were trying not to kill each other.

I let her sew you and me matching red georgette frocks – yours has a smocked bodice and mine has puffy sleeves. But on the day of the celebration, she lets me put you in a soft cotton all-in-one before she dresses you.

Our kitchen table is covered with plates and bowls of food your Grand Mar has cooked. There is no lobster or crab, but there are massive prawns and whole steamed fish. Bowls of red eggs and ginger, noodles, glutinous rice nestled in banana leaves.

"It would have been difficult to take a new baby out to a restaurant anyway," your Grand Mar tells me. But I reckon it's because she was too proud to ask your Grand Par.

This is the first time anyone apart from your Grand Par and the community service workers has ever set foot in our flat. "Such a good idea, celebrating a baby's first hundred days instead of first year," says Mrs Osman, holding a spring roll wrapped in a serviette. "One of our Korea customer tell me she done the same thing." Her husband, the short, silent man holding her handbag, simply nods. Your Grand Mar has invited Aunt Yenny and her family too, but only Aunt Yenny comes. "Winsome and the boys are too busy at the restaurant," she half-apologises.

Then your Grand Par arrives, carrying a slab of beer. When I open the door, there's a girl standing next to him in a white eyelet lace dress and sandals. She's small, the size I was when I was thirteen, and for a moment I think that your Grand Par has brought along his other secret daughter. But then I see that her eyes are old and guarded, and your Grand Par's arm is circling her round hips. She's a woman, a woman smiling at me with her teeth only.

"This is Lan," says your Grand Par. "Lan, this is my daughter, Karuna."

He looks from Lan to me, and then back again. His eyes glitter: he's proud of his tall daughter and his young girlfriend. I bet he is thinking we could almost be sisters, because that is what I am thinking.

Lan dips out her tiny hand with pink nails, like a Shih Tzu offering her paw.

I don't take it.

"Come in," I tell them.

Your Grand Mar is on the sofa, holding you. She looks up and sees your Grand Par and Lan. There is no surprise on her face. Looking back down at you, she chucks your chin and ignores them both.

"Lan got you a present," your Grand Par tells me.

"Umm, thanks." I take the small wrapped package that he hands me, but don't unwrap it. I just watch as the two of them head over to the food table, and your Grand Par fusses over Lan in a way he's never fussed over your Grand Mar or me. Pretty soon he's heaped a mountain of food on a paper plate for her, and cracked open a beer for himself.

I'm suddenly embarrassed for your Grand Mar. She's invited the only friends she has, who also happen to be her employers. I bet she wasn't expecting Grand Par to bring along a "friend". She probably thought he'd come alone, and they'd be separate but doting grandparents.

Your Grand Par and Lan spend half the afternoon canoodling on the couch, as he drains can after can from the slab that no one else touches.

Your Grand Mar ignores them the entire time. "Come to Mar," she coos at you over your cradle. "Sweet, small pup, so clever, already winking at your Mar!"

"Why do you say that?" demands your Grand Par, suddenly looking her way.

She glares at him like he's demented.

"Ha, you the *mother*?" Your Grand Par is shouting now, a crazy glint in his eye. "You? You're going to pretend that she's yours now? You old hag, who would knock you up? You don't even have eyebrows!"

He's a mean drunk, your Grand Par. I suddenly see that how much he loved me as a little girl is directly inverse to how much he will love me as an adult woman. It is hard to be a tool kitty when you are sixteen turning seventeen; hard for your father to call you that and not feel icky about it. It's also hard to watch a young woman sitting on your father's lap, and your father petting her like a toy. So *she's* the reason he's moving to Wodonga.

"It also mean Grandma, you idiot," your Grand Mar hisses. "How dare you come in and insult me in front of our guests. Get out of my house."

"No. I paid for all this food!"

"Get out."

"Karuna wants me here." He gulps from his can. "She's my daughter too. I'm a grandfather now."

I wonder how Lan feels about dating a grandfather.

"How much of a grandfather you be since this baby born, huh?"

"Ha ha. I've been gone fer only two years and you can't even make sure she doesn't get knocked up!"

I watch your Grand Mar and Grand Par, a decade of hatred strung tight between them like those tin-can telephones I made as a kid – the further apart they drift, the stronger the decibels.

I am glad that your dad is not around, doesn't even know you exist, because it means that we would never come to this, and you would never see love turned inside out like a sock peeled from a bleeding foot.

"Shut up!" a new voice cries. We all turn to look at Mrs Osman. At that moment you let out a howl. "You're both scaring the baby." Mrs Osman wrests you from your Grand Mar's arms and hands you to me. "Maybe she's hungry. Go to quiet place and feed her."

I close the door to our bedroom, muffling the adult show of sound and fury. I sit on the bed for what seems like a gentle eternity, nursing you. Your eyes roll back like you are slowly dying of contentment. To think I could bring such satisfaction to a creature.

Eventually there is a knock at the bedroom door. Probably Mrs Osman coming to check on me.

But it's not.

"Tweezer!"

She has somehow entered our flat, greeted all the warring adults and made it to the bedroom with such soft, mousey quietness that I get the shock of my life.

"Your mother invited me," Tweezer explains, "and Adisa helped me get here. She's still in the lounge room talking to your mum."

"What's happening out there?" I ask. "Is it still mayhem?"

"Mayhem?"

"Are my dad and his girlfriend still there?"

"We saw them on our way up here," Tweezer told me, "if you mean your dad and your cousin."

"That wasn't my cousin. Trust me, you don't want to know."

I can see Tweezer trying her best not to look at me with my boob out, trying to find a safe landing spot for her eyes that will not invade the privacy of our bedroom either.

I help her out. "So, Tweezer," I say, "you've learned to lie to your mum and dad."

She looks down at the floor. "I had to. There was no way they were going to let me come here."

"Good on you."

A little smile skids across her face.

You unlatch yourself from me, fling your head back and sigh a little *ahhh*.

"Oh, can I hold her?" Tweezer asks.

"Yeah, come sit on the bed."

I hand you over and she looks down at your sleeping face with the same melted expression that I hoped and dreamed my best friend would have, and all is forgiven.

"Hi, youse all." Standing at the door is Adisa, wearing a bubble-skirt dress with a pattern on it that could either be birds or banana peels. "Whatcha doin'?" She plonks herself down next to Tweezer and looks at you. "She's perfect," she declares. She pokes her pointer finger into your clenched fist. "Oooh. So tiny. I've never seen a hand so small before. So strong! Can I have a go at holding her?"

But Tweezer won't let go of you. Adisa laughs, a deep, furry laugh. I like it. I know for sure, without even asking, that coming here was Adisa's idea. Tweezer would have just mentioned it to her as an impossibility, and Adisa would've been the one to hatch the plan, to think up the lie. She's good for Tweezer, I think. In fact, if she had been at school while I was there, I might have pinched her for myself, and Tweezer wouldn't have been able to put up a fight. The thought makes me smile. Poor Tweezer.

"Thanks for the ring," I tell Adisa. "I really appreciated it."

"Ha!" she scoffs. "You're welcome, my friend. But you're not wearing it, so it probably means that your mum thought it was a cheap piece of shit and chucked it away."

I am flabbergasted.

She grins. "When I told my mum, she laughed at my dumb-arse idea about protecting your honour, and told me I was an embarrassment to society." Yet there's no bitterness or malice when Adisa says this, only affection, which makes me realise she has a very different relationship with her mother than Tweezer and I do with ours. "She also told me to tell you that you shouldn't need to get hitched to get respect."

"Adisa's mum's a legend," says Tweezer.

"She's a dag," says Adisa, but I can tell she agrees entirely with Tweezer.

We sit in silence for a while, thinking about our mums.

Your hand shoots up to rub your eye, and that's when I remember that I am one too.

Sitting next to two teenagers at a party with my arms free, for a moment I had forgotten.

Mrs Osman helps your Grand Mar pack the leftover food into plastic containers donated by Aunt Yenny. "Well, that was success," she comments. She had told her husband to go home, that she would catch the bus later.

"No, it wasn't," laments your Grand Mar. "Karuna's no-good father come only to show off that fresh-off-boat girl."

Mrs Osman arches her black-pencil eyebrow and continues scooping noodles into a clear box. "It was success. Karuna's friends come. Your other lady boss come. He pay for all this food that we cleaning up. But when they go home, she cleaning up his vomit. You win!"

Your Grand Mar chuckles. But she still won't let it go. As she clears your Grand Par's beer cans from the coffee table, she complains to Mrs Osman. "Her no-good father always get her to do dangerous things in the garage, make her crawl under those junk cars, let her pass him heavy tools. I always telling him, one day your shonky chain hoist will break and she be squashed by a cheap Datsun."

Then she turns to me, speaking our language. "Remember the afternoon he whacked your chin with the wrench? The scar is still there, I've never forgiven him. 'She's just a girl!' I used to yell at him, 'She can't do this dirty work,' and you would get pissed off at me and lift your scar-chin and stomp around like a little bulldog, like *I* was the one trying to hurt you."

Your Grand Mar ties the tops of two large garbage bags. "I take downstairs," she tells Mrs Osman.

I wipe the coffee table while Mrs Osman holds you and coos at you. "So perfect, little one." She sighs. I brace myself for her mentioning her lost baby, but she doesn't. Instead, she tells me, "It's shame your mother's parents cannot see this little beauty. Maybe if they see your baby, they start talk to her again."

"They can't," I reply. "They're dead."

Mrs Osman looks at me funny, like I've used the Lord's name in vain without meaning to. "What you mean, they dead?"

"They died before I was born."

"No. They in the Philippines."

"No, they're not."

"Yes, they are! They alive. She talk about them all the time to me."

"She told me they were dead."

"No, no, no. They living with her sister in the Philippines, but not talking with her for seventeen years, after she run away with your father."

Mrs Osman chuckles. "Your mother was very naughty when she young, no?"

*

That evening after dinner, I say that Mrs Osman thinks I have grandparents still living in the Philippines. I expect your Grand Mar to call Mrs Osman a liar but she simply says, "That's true."

"What? How come you said they were dead?"

"Because," sighs your Grand Mar, "they are like dead to me. What's the difference? My own mother's last words to me were, 'If you leave, then don't bother showing your face here again. You will be no better than those girls who buzz around the foreign soldiers.' They disowned me, so now I have nothing to do with them. My sister Lee Lee was always their favourite anyway. She ended up marrying a watch repairman and having six kids, and they're always waiting for the handouts I send from Australia."

I think about the sample packets of condoms – her sister Lee Lee could have used them earlier.

"If you think I'm mean to you," your Grand Mar tells me, "when I met your Grand Par, my own mother told me, 'Those White Ghosts have low standards, they think we all look the same.' Meaning that your Grand Par couldn't tell an Asian woman with the face of a donkey apart from an Asian woman with the face of a *binukot*. So when I had you, I couldn't believe that someone like me had made something like you – so white, so perfect, more beautiful than all your skinny-arse cousins back home. But your grandparents didn't even want to meet you." She sighs.

Your Grand Mar saw me as her little shooting star, this girl who could have her pick of all the successful men in our small world. She had dressed me up and made me up, chaperoned me and chased away unworthy distractions. And I had unwittingly chosen well, chosen a man who was going places. But unlike her, I had not clung to him as my way out of a dead-end.

Oddly enough, since you were born she's stopped bugging me so much about your father. Maybe she just assumes he's a deadbeat who'll never be able to pay child support. Or maybe she doesn't want anything else to disrupt our little self-contained trinity. We are the only family she has now, this small brown woman adrift in a world of Ghosts and half-Ghosts. When she looks into your tiny brown face she probably sees something more familiar, closer to home, than my own face.

"By the way, there's a letter for you," she tells me. "I'm not sure whether it's junk mail from your dad's magazine. Usually they're addressed to him, but this one has your name on it. He's probably managed to forward the bill our way."

She hands me the still unopened letter. *Miss K. Kelly*. I've never received mail before, and the moment I recognise the flying horse logo, my heart beats faster.

I open the envelope and unfold the letter, scanning the short paragraph before a smaller slip of paper falls loose – a cheque!

"It's not junk mail," I say.

"Is it the joke?" she asks.

"Huh?"

"You said you'd write a joke to win a hundred dollars."

"It's not a joke, Mar, but I did win some money."

"How much?"

"Two hundred dollars."

"Come on, you're joking now." I show her the cheque. "Be careful," she tells me, "it must be fake. Who gives you two hundred dollars for nothing?"

"It's not fake. I earned it. I wrote a story and sent it in, and the letter says it will get printed in next year's summer issue."

She doesn't snatch the cheque out of my hands but stares at it to double-check that yes, my name appears on the first dotted line and yes, I have indeed made this small fortune, almost as much as my entire time working at the salon.

"This is real?"

"Yes! The letter says so."

Your Grand Mar has never once told me that she loves me, or that anything I've ever accomplished is any good. She has only ever given me instructions or criticism. But that moment, she looks at me with absolute wonder, amazed that I've managed to pull off such a stunt. I recognise that look for what it is, and I will never forget it: she is wildly proud of me.

And I did it all as a free agent, behind her back.

"On Monday we'll go into town," she decides. "To the bank, so you can open a new account for this cheque. You can also bank that one hundred dollars your dad gave you. Also, if you have your own account I think the government will give you some support money for the baby if you apply for it. Which you should."

Your Grand Mar and I – we have been like two puzzles that someone dropped on the floor. We didn't know which bits belonged where. We were too frantic putting ourselves back together again that we just grabbed at pieces of each other. We were hasty, pressing our sharp corners down whether they fitted or not.

In our efforts to find ourselves, we knew no boundaries. By locking me up, your Grand Mar thought she was keeping the good part of herself safe at home, getting the rest and respite she'd always yearned for, vicariously, through me. She thought she was spoiling me, in a way. But I have to get back into the world. I think about that peeling poster on the wall of the community centre. *Life. Be in it.*

I know that when I am back at school next year and she is minding you, I will not be able to hear what she might make you call her when you start to talk, or see where she will take you when you start to walk. Yet I hope that she might realise, this second time around, that love is not all about control. She loves you as much as I love you, but you are our visitor from tomorrow and neither of us can claim you.

You are the song of yourself.

Epilogue

When summer rolls around again, your Grand Mar suggests I go back to the government house for the free tutoring program. "And this time, stick to it," she says. "If you'd stuck to it last time, you wouldn't have got yourself into trouble." Ha.

But I don't go to High School Survival Tools that summer. I don't go back to check if your father's teaching Homework Help. I don't go back searching for the Once that started this Upon a Time.

I spend it with you, watching you discover each sense and limb. When you stretch your jaw, your eyebrows shoot up. When you smile, your eyes turn into little crescent moons. I am there the day when, after waving your arms in front of your face, you suddenly notice one hand like a paused windscreen wiper, and you stare and stare. I am there when you can grasp my finger and pull it to your gummy-shark mouth.

And when the school year starts, I re-enrol in Corindirk High School. Legally, I could have left, and Mrs Osman has offered me a full-time job, but I know I'm not cut out for hairdressing. I also know how lucky I am – if Tweezer had got knocked up, I'm not sure her parents would have let her go back to school.

But that's not to say I enjoy it. I treat it like a job, because I must. Your Grand Mar no longer works at Mrs Osman's because she looks after you during the day, so I have to take this seriously. I sit in class, do my work and leave to take over from your Grand Mar while she goes to her shift at Siamese Please. This isn't any special high-school program for teenage mums. This is just ordinary high school, and until I had you, I didn't realise just how *ordinary* it really was. All those teenagers, worrying about how they look and what they said and who they were with when they said it. What seems like landmines in their adolescence are to me just little potholes. So of course, they still think I'm up myself, but I don't care what they think. Thoughts change a million times a week.

One afternoon during the Easter holidays your Grand Mar is minding you while I take a walk around the block, and that's when I see it. Your father's car, in the community centre car park, a solid silver wink between the Datsuns and Fords.

He is back.

I could just walk past, but I can't help myself.

I go into the building, thinking I'll just glance through the small window on the door of his classroom.

But I can't see very much, so I enter.

And there he is, your dad who doesn't know he's your dad, head bent over a desk, helping some kid with a worksheet.

He looks up at me, and a big smile spreads across his face. "Hey, you!"

I seem to be the same creature I was a year ago: same flannel shirt, same leggings. There's no clue that anything as major as another human being has happened to me.

But *he* is different.

It is a shock just how different. He looks much younger than I remember. To think that only a year ago I had thought he was an Older Man! He walks from behind the front desk and I notice how jaunty his stride is, none of the languid lingering he did last summer.

I remember my little make-believe ending all those months ago when I first fantasised that you existed, before I knew for sure – how your dad would return and I'd reveal you to him, his marshmallow-cheeked miracle, and he'd be all teary and drop down on one knee and pledge his forever-love.

I had been imagining a very different young man.

"How was Adelaide?" I ask him.

"Adelaide's a hole," he laughs. "There's *nothing* to do there. Churches take up the whole city where the fun places are supposed to be. I think I must've gone to twenty movies last year. There was nothing else to do. Oh, and I drank a bit. The pubs are good."

Then, as an afterthought, he adds, "What did *you* do?" He asks in a tone that does not expect a reply longer than two or three words.

I had a baby, I could have said.

I had your baby, I could have told him.

I worked in a beauty salon for three months. I walked for four hours every day for a week, carrying five litres of water inside me. I ate boiled watermelon. I tried to escape from a fourteenth-floor window.

But I give him what he asks for, because I know he cannot see me any other way. I was his little handmaiden up in the cardboard commission flat. What I'd done all year in his mind was to exist in my dad's old flannels, waiting for the rock star to return with his heated car seats.

"Not much."

"How's school for you?"

"Okay."

"Hey, I missed you," he tells me. "Did you miss me?"

"Hey, Ray, I'm stuck on this page."

"Just a moment, Vinny, I'm talking to Karuna."

"Agghh."

"Just move onto the next page, I'll be there in a sec."

He has forgotten the rest of the students. This whole session seems like a public performance between him and me.

"I can't do the next page until I get this one!" Vinny protests.

It must be so good to be the sun around which everything revolves. He's a boy who likes to be liked.

And I know he still likes me, but the burning summer in my bloodstream has gone.

"Wait, don't go yet, I'll give you a lift when I'm done," he offers.

I have only missed an idea of him, I realise. He left me with an image so full of holes that my mind filled in the gaps, but now I discover I'd coloured him in all wrong. Wasted all the expensive gold paint on something that was only supposed to be blue or green.

Where it had once enchanted me, his goofiness now annoys me. His way of speaking, his way of dropping words like they don't mean anything because there are always ears willing to listen. He doesn't need to save up all the things he needs to say, and then hope that someone will hear him.

"Nah. It's okay," I reply.

"Come on," he insists, thinking that I'm just being polite, his little ghetto girl.

"No, thanks. I'm happy to walk."

"Want some company? I'll walk with you."

"No. It's okay."

He's surprised. Surprised that I've refused his offer. Surprised that I don't want to resume where we left off.

But I've only come to say hello.

And goodbye.

The drop of golden sun has evaporated.

"So, did you end up reading the Whitman?" he asks, finally.

Your father believes that a book he took from a free junk pile and gifted me is what has preoccupied me all year, outside my adolescent school life. He has absolutely no knowledge of his other, far greater gift.

He may have a special life all set out for him, but now so do I. There's been a hit song this year, a bouncy tune about being guilty of love in the first degree. I did fall in love. Just not with Ray.

I met somebody new.

Ray might never know such misery or boredom or days without hope, days that end where they begin, days that stretch on and on, and days that disappear with a few long naps. He will never know what it is like to have others assume you've wasted your life when you start growing a new life at an age they deem obscene, to have your existence feel like an inconvenience to others.

But I never made myself smaller. I couldn't. I had to justify our existence. The moment I saw you, a bloody astronaut tethered to this mothership, I knew my universe had shifted. True, your father was the sort of boy who might never know one hundred days of isolation, but he would never know such hard-won joy either.

"I did," I reply.

I celebrate myself.

Acknowledgements

Thank you to my excellent editors, Chris Feik and Jo Rosenberg, to the entire team at Black Inc., and to my wonderful agents Clare Forster and Catherine Drayton. Thank you to Sophy Williams and Gabriella Page-Fort, for bringing my book to US readers.

ALICE PUNG is an award-winning writer based in Melbourne. She is the bestselling author of the memoirs *Unpolished Gem* and *Her Father's Daughter*, and the essay collection *Close to Home*, as well as the editor of the anthologies *Growing up Asian in Australia* and *My First Lesson*. Her first novel, *Laurinda*, won the Ethel Turner Prize at the 2016 NSW Premier's Literary Awards.

Here ends Alice Pung's
One Hundred Days.

The first edition of this book was printed
and bound at Lakeside Book Company in
Harrisonburg, Virginia, in September 2023.

A NOTE ON THE TYPE

The text of this novel was set in Adobe Caslon, a
typeface inspired by the original Caslon serif type-
faces designed in 1722 by William Caslon. Caslon's
types were based on seventeenth-century Dutch old-
style designs, which were then used extensively in
England. Because of their practicality, Caslon's designs met with instant success. The first printings of
the American Declaration of Independence and the
Constitution were set in Caslon. The Adobe Caslon
is a revival of the original font designed by Carol
Twombly.

HARPERVIA

An imprint dedicated to publishing international voices,
offering readers a chance to encounter other lives and other
points of view via the language of the imagination.